Death in

Comanche County

Linda McDonald

Table of Contents

CHAPTER ONE	8
CHAPTER TWO	15
CHAPTER THREE	19
CHAPTER FOUR	27
CHAPTER FIVE	34
CHAPTER SIX	37
CHAPTER SEVEN	41
CHAPTER EIGHT	46
CHAPTER NINE	51
CHAPTER TEN	57
CHAPTER ELEVEN	65
CHAPTER TWELVE	71
CHAPTER THIRTEEN	81
CHAPTER FOURTEEN	89
CHAPTER FIFTEEN	100
CHAPTER SIXTEEN	106
CHAPTER SEVENTEEN	111
CHAPTER EIGHTEEN	118
CHAPTER NINETEEN	119
CHAPTER TWENTY	126
CHAPTER TWENTY-ONE	130

CHAPTER TWENTY-TWO	134
CHAPTER TWENTY-THREE	139
CHAPTER TWENTY-FOUR	143
CHAPTER TWENTY-FIVE	146
CHAPTER TWENTY-SIX	151
CHAPTER TWENTY-SEVEN	154
CHAPTER TWENTY-EIGHT	162
CHAPTER TWENTY-NINE	169
CHAPTER THIRTY	173
CHAPTER THIRTY-ONE	176
CHAPTER THIRTY-TWO	184
CHAPTER THIRTY-THREE	188
CHAPTER THIRTY-FOUR	198
CHAPTER THIRTY-FIVE	203
CHAPTER THIRTY-SIX	208
CHAPTER THIRTY-SEVEN	214
CHAPTER THIRTY-EIGHT	218
CHAPTER THIRTY-NINE	220
CHAPTER FORTY	227
CHAPTER FORTY-ONE	232
CHAPTER FORTY-TWO	234
CHAPTER FORTY-THREE	237

CHAPTER FORTY-FOUR	239
CHAPTER FORTY-FIVE	243
CHAPTER FORTY-SIX	245
CHAPTER FORTY-SEVEN	249
CHAPTER FORTY-EIGHT	252
CHAPTER FORTY-NINE	255
CHAPTER FIFTY	258
CHAPTER FIFTY-ONE	263
CHAPTER FIFTY-TWO	266
CHAPTER FIFTY-THREE	270
CHAPTER FIFTY-FOUR	272
READER REVIEWS	277

CHAPTER ONE

A yellow security light hits a cluster of evergreens, turning them amber. Inside their circle, the orange tip of a cigarette glows for a moment in the darkness. Seconds later, it drops to the ground and disappears.

Stepping out of the shadows, a man in all black pulls a woman's stocking over his head. He slips on blue latex gloves and checks his weapon, a metallic red knife, its thin, short blade as lethal as a straight razor.

His work boots, shrouded in clear plastic tied up around the ankles, move with stealth through the dead leaves to the chain-link, perimeter fence surrounding Medicine Wheel R.V. Village.

Save for a light breeze, the park lies still, its inhabitants asleep, only a few porch lights shining. Using bolt cutters, he snips an opening in the fence. As he slides through the break, the night sky streaks with light. A barrage of artillery shells explodes.

The man jumps and crouches, his heart pulsating like a machine gun. Dogs bark and howl all around the park. After a moment, he calms down and stands back up, chiding himself.

Fort Sill, a military reservation in Medicine Wheel's back yard, performs routine artillery training drills that can unnerve the sturdiest if they don't know what's going on. It feels like someone is dropping bombs right on top of you. Usually, locals pause for a second at the sound of the maneuvers, then go about their business.

The man's tightly strung tonight, though, so it takes some effort to steady himself. He moves ahead, slipping through the darkness toward his target, a 40' Gulfstream mobile home with a single light over the back entrance.

He easily picks the back door lock and listens. Hearing nothing inside, the intruder slips into the living area. A night light barely illuminates the walls, dominated by framed photographs and Christian crosses—from homemade ones to gilded, carved creations. Over the sofa hangs a Bible-story-type painting of a blond Jesus with children on his lap.

The wall pictures illustrate a long nursing career—a young brunette in a nurse's uniform shows off a diploma, smiles beside patients' beds, blows out birthday candles, and poses on vacation in front of European cathedrals.

Silently scoffing at the religious collections, the man opens the drawers of a side table and rifles through a sheaf of papers under the halo of a tiny penlight he holds in his teeth. Pausing to check for other sounds, he systematically sweeps every drawer and counter. The only sound is the whispered crunch of the plastic covering his boots.

A slight rustle from down the hall makes him freeze. Snapping off the penlight, he perspires inside his hosiery mask. He knew if he got what he was there for, he might get lucky, and she would sleep through it. But he hadn't expected a confrontation this soon.

Effie Lawrence, a bird-like lady of seventy, comes down the hallway into the kitchen area, which adjoins the living room. In the darkness, she fills a glass with tap water and stands drinking it over the sink, looking out into the woods behind her place.

She stiffens suddenly and goes still. Effie senses rather than sees the intruder and realizes what woke her up. Her body shifts into full alert mode.

Outside, a dog howls at a paltry slice of moon. Effie steadies herself, gripping the counter with her other hand. Even though her legs feel like they might give way beneath her, she slowly turns her head toward the living area.

As her vision adjusts to the darkness, she can see piles of papers spread over the floor, though she can't make out the dark shape hovering over them.

Effie Lawrence has always known this night could come. It's just that it all happened so many years ago, the details blur in her mind now. Even though she has prepared herself, now that it has arrived, she still feels shocked.

Like her father's lingering death from an illness that the family had long since accepted as fatal. Yet, the last cruel surge still left them all stunned, unprepared for the mortal blow.

Now she can only do what she has rehearsed in her head a thousand times. Calming herself as best she can, Effie puts the glass down on the counter and starts back toward her bedroom. Her loaded .22 is in there, clean and checked, even though she hasn't fired it in years.

She barely makes it to the hallway before a blue-latex hand clamps onto her upper arm. It squeezes so hard she cries out.

"Shhh," the intruder rasps. "Make a sound and you're

dead."

Effie thinks she might know the voice but is too addled to be sure. She looks into the face, but the features are too distorted by a pantyhose mask.

"Where is it?" He speaks in a coarse whisper, as if to disguise his voice.

"What?"

He jerks her arm again by way of answer. "Give it to me, and I won't have to junk your whole place."

"Give you what?"

"Don't play dumb. Where's your safe?"

"I don't have a safe."

His fist slams into her jaw. Effie stumbles and nearly falls from the force of the blow. Her ears ring. She knows she is not strong enough to take another punch like that and stay on her feet.

She prays silently. *Dear Lord, be with me now in my hour of need.*

"Where are your valuables?" His voice is an ugly hiss by now.

Motioning toward the bedroom, she whispers, "Cedar chest."

He drags her down the hall into her bedroom and pushes her down in front of the elegant chest that once held her dowry. The latch is locked.

"Open it."

Effie tries to shake off dizziness as she gets the key from her jewelry box. She unlocks the Lane chest sitting at the foot of her bed.

The intruder pushes her back into a chair before rifling the contents.

He opens some old ring boxes and tosses them to the floor. He quickly pockets a roll of cash. The rest of her things—family keepsakes, her own baby shoes, scrapbooks—he flings to the side. Then she hears his pleased sigh as legal folders appear under the personal contents.

Effie Lawrence can only watch as someone else's filthy hands toss around the stuff of her life. She could tell him that what he is after isn't there but knows he won't believe her. It is cold comfort now to realize that she had been right to secure it elsewhere.

She holds onto the crucifix around her neck, watching him empty the cedar chest, sensing something familiar about his body movements.

Then his distorted face turns on her. "Listen, old lady. You've either got it, or you got the money. Which is it?"

"I burned it."

He erupts. "No, you're not that fucking stupid." He takes a second and lowers his voice again. "Else I wouldn't be here."

"You'll never find it. I don't even know where it is any more." Her voice sounds far away to her, as though it's no longer coming out of her body.

He yanks her up out of the chair. She can feel the anger pouring out of him, in sour fumes and cigarette breath—a biblical fury.

"I'll start with cutting off your toes," he whispers. "You understand? That will only be the beginning."

Effie knows he means it. She thinks about the gun in her nightstand, a world away now. She had comforted herself earlier with the fact that he was wearing a mask. It might mean he didn't plan to kill her.

Now her heart drops. She understands he will hurt her first. Nothing quick or simple.

Part of her understands it is over. For the first time in decades, she asks herself if it was worth it. But she prayed for guidance all those years ago, and when it came, she made her promises to God. She clutches her crucifix and looks at the remains of her life thrown on the floor.

It all seems pointless now. It was so long ago. But it is more than her now, whose life is at stake. Still, Effie Lawrence keeps her promises. The Hereafter depends on it.

The wind picks up outside.

The intruder's hand darts into his pocket. Then he snaps the deadly knife open.

Effie wants to close her eyes but can't. *Thy will, not mine, be done.*

But then her bedside lamp shines through his nylon mask, just so, and Effie sees who it is.

She gasps.

"Oh, Lord, you? No, no, it can't . . . but why?" Effie has no idea why he, of all people, wants to kill her.

CHAPTER TWO

Music swells as a terrified, voluptuous peasant in a ripped corset stumbles through a black forest of trees.

"Help me. Someone. Help, help."

Panting on her heels, a half-wolf man slices his straight razor wildly through the air. She trips and falls, screaming, trying to scoot away from him. His hairy hand lifts the blade high in the moonlight and strikes.

High-pitched *Psycho* stabbing sounds yank Cheryl Jackson out of a sweat-soaked sleep. Heart racing, she manages to get one eye open. The other feels glued shut.

It takes a moment to realize she's lying in her recliner. A dried-up Mac-N-Cheese frozen dinner sits in her lap.

Feeling for the remote on the arm rest, she grabs it and lowers the volume on the T.V. She grits her teeth and gingerly pulls the recliner's handle into the upright position. A shooting pain in her head makes her freeze.

She must have passed out here last night. Staring out one throbbing eye at the T.V., she sees the maniac wolf-man hack away at his screaming prey. She closes her eyes to concentrate. What on earth went on here? It's a blank.

At thirty-five, Cheryl knows better. Yet here she is again, eyelids undulating as alcohol vapors rumble through her veins. Trying to get her bearings, Cheryl looks around the walls of her mobile home.

A picture of the Medicine Wheel Hotel lobby flashes into her head. A window there works as a convenient, if unofficial, post office. It's right across the hall from the hotel's popular bar.

Cheryl can't remember if she did a mail run there last night. Handling clients' mail is one of the many odd jobs that generate her income. In an R.V. park occupied largely by the retired, chores like shopping, cleaning, transportation, and lawn work always need doing.

If she limits her own shopping to Dollar General and discount stores, Cheryl can maintain a comfortable, Early-Poverty lifestyle. Hardly what she once dreamed for herself, but that ship sailed long ago.

A second flash—sitting under a Budweiser neon sign, a shot glass in front of her. Cheryl can almost feel the warm amber liquid caressing her throat like a lover, sliding down like honey. Her memory abruptly cuts out again.

On the television a Nomad car phone commercial soars over the tympani drums of the *2001: A Space Odyssey* theme. In 1989, the only people in Medicine Wheel to have Nomads—at $1495 apiece—are law enforcement.

Cheryl turns off the T.V. and braces herself to get up from the recliner. The Mac-N-Cheese spills to the floor, spewing cracked orange particles onto the carpet.

"Damn it," she mutters, but knows better than to bend over yet to pick them up. Her head still threatens to explode, and her bad leg feels almost numb. She stands a second before putting weight on it. Discarded clothes in front of her catch her attention: turtleneck, jeans, and underwear lie scattered in a path to the bedroom.

A rancid taste pops up in her mouth. *Tell me I didn't. Oh God, just shoot me.*

She cringes as the image of Doyle Lowe, in his bomber jacket and tight jeans, grinning at her from a barstool. Now an older, tired version of the former All-State halfback, he still has those half-lidded eyes that suck her in. *Come on, you know you want to.*

That's the problem. She often does want to. It horrifies her that she finds any part of him still charming. But why else can he set her humming when she runs into him? They had been married maybe twenty minutes before she caught him in bed with a cheerleader. The divorce was just as quick.

Still, almost ten years later, she can barely manage a civil hello to him on the street without bristling. Doyle never left Medicine Wheel, but stays a perennial fixture, a constant reminder of their joke of a marriage. And the sensual pull he still has on her.

Stumbling to the window, she's relieved to see her pickup, yet it also upsets her. She has a firm rule about driving after even one drink.

Her last DUI conviction in Oklahoma City had finally slapped a deep scare into her. Cheryl's escape to a teaching career in the city had ended abruptly when she wrapped her car around a telephone pole one evening and nearly lost her right leg. The long, hard party with alcohol was over.

It marked the beginning of sober meetings and led to two

years sobriety. Yet, a few months ago she had picked up a drink again. Why she did it, she still doesn't know. It makes her feel ashamed and small, screwing up the one thing besides playing basketball that she ever got right. Now it's tougher than ever to go without a drink. *I have seriously got to get myself to a meeting.*

As she mentally flogs herself, the shrill ring of the phone shatters the stillness. She picks up the receiver and feels something crusty all over it, like someone was pawing down peanuts while they talked on it.

Please tell me I didn't start drunk-dialing long distance last night. I must've been totally hammered.

CHAPTER THREE

Staring across Turquoise Lane, the street that runs between his mobile home and Cheryl's, Silas Weintraub grips his phone and taps his foot impatiently, waiting to see if she will answer. Probably back on the sauce, he thinks on the third ring.

It saddens and infuriates him. Usually, he has no patience for people pissing their lives away on alcohol, but something about Cheryl softens his leathery old heart.

He could just cross the street and knock on the door until she rouses herself, but damn it all, she promised to call him at 9:00 sharp. It's almost 9:30, and he's cranking on his third mug of coffee, two more than Doc Weathers says he can have. Not that doctors hold much sway in his life. By all rights, Silas should be long dead.

Her gravelly voice finally answers. "Hello, Cheryl's Personal Services . . .."

Silas interrupts her spiel. "Cheryl, up and at 'em. You were going to be here a half hour ago with Effie's list."

"Oh, crap, Walmart day. Sorry, Silas, overslept."

"Typical," he snorts. "Well, put a move on it. I'll bring you some coffee." Even though it's Sunday, he and Cheryl will drive into Lawton to do their weekly Walmart run. They always have the store to themselves then. Everybody else is in church.

"Just give me a minute," she says.

He squints out the window of his place and is surprised Effie isn't already at work in her yard. Usually by this time, the old gal is watering and fussing over her pots of chrysanthemums before cleaning up for church. Next door, in stark contrast, Cheryl's disaster of a yard needs a tractor.

As is the garden, so is the gardener, Silas remembers his mother saying, usually clucking her teeth over some lazy neighbor's yard. He pours an extra mug of black coffee and heads across the street.

Silas's squat, trunk-like torso rocks from side to side as he paces outside her front door, holding the coffees. He wears his usual tossup of clothes—today a chartreuse sweater with a hole in it and gray slacks—his white hair naturally scruffy. At 78, he is no longer the Polish businessman of his youth, but an old man who wears whatever he damn well feels like throwing on.

Cheryl finally emerges in jeans and sweater, her face still puffy with sleep. He doesn't ask, just shakes his head. "You look like you haven't gone to bed. You got Effie's list?"

She has no witty response, just takes the offered coffee. "She was still adding stuff to it yesterday afternoon. She said she'd tape it to the door." Cheryl heads that way, but Silas pushes ahead of her.

"Never mind," he says, hoofing it toward Effie's door. "I'll get it."

Of course, it isn't just Cheryl's lateness that sends him

hurrying to Effie's door. Anybody with half a brain knows Silas Weintraub has been in love with the woman for years. The only question is why they haven't managed to officially get together, since the feeling seems to be mutual. It could be Silas's disdain for organized religion, or Effie's distrust of anyone not religious . . . except for Silas, whom she excuses. Even Effie agrees that anyone who survived Auschwitz gets a pass. At any rate, Silas can play at being indignant or disappointed in Cheryl all he wants. His quick steps to Effie's door are about having a good excuse to see her himself.

There's no list taped to her door. By the time Cheryl catches up, he is still waiting for his knock to be answered, which is odd. Effie is usually quick to get the door.

"Effie? Effie, you in there? It's Silas and Cheryl. We're headed to Walmart. Need your list." He looks at Cheryl with a question mark.

Cheryl shrugs her shoulders and joins in, as if it might make a difference who calls for her.

"Effie? You in there?"

They look at one another, growing uneasy at the same time. Something's not right.

Silas feels a lead ball drop into his stomach, an omen he experienced almost daily in the death camps, as word of new fatalities spread through the grapevine.

"Dammit, Effie." He jiggles the doorknob.

Cheryl glances around at the back driveway. "Her car's here."

Silas presses his face against the front window. As he sees the living area inside, a rattle passes through his throat.

"What is it?" Over his shoulder, Cheryl looks inside, too. "Oh no. No."

Silas suddenly finds the fury of a man thirty years younger. He throws his shoulder into the door to break it down. It doesn't give.

"Wait, Silas. I have her key." Her shaky fingers fumble through the key ring and find it.

As she pushes the door open, he steps in front and instinctively puts his arm up to block her, as if to spare her the sight. But he's too late.

They both stand there for a moment, unbelieving. The room has been ransacked, a sea of scattered papers, furniture gutted, drawer contents thrown all over the carpet.

"How could I not have heard this?" Cheryl shifts her attention toward the hall to the bedroom. "Effie?" The name echoes.

Silas feels acid rise up into his mouth, a sense of disaster rushing through him. He hurries down the hall, his legs seeming to move without his bidding.

When he sees the bedroom, a tortured wail shoots up his spine. If the living room was a storm of torn up furniture and papers, Effie's lilac-themed bedroom is a sea of red gashes and spatter . . . on the walls, the carpet, and the bed. Blood lies in dark congealed pools in the mattress, which is slashed to pieces. It looks like a grotesque abstract painting.

Effie's body lies, twisted unnaturally onto its side, by the bed, as if someone had carelessly dropped her there. Her neck and chest are sliced with stab wounds.

Cheryl comes in behind Silas and has to steady herself in the door frame. She swoons and reaches for a corner of the dresser. Her hand comes down on something sticky. With a moan, she realizes that a bit of blood has pooled on the dresser top.

"Oh my god," she whispers. She holds her stained hand out, as though she doesn't know what to do with it.

"You okay?" Silas manages, looking up from kneeling beside Effie.

"Yeah." Cheryl reaches for a tissue from the dresser and wipes her hand. Then, shaking her head at the horrific sight, she kneels beside Silas.

Silas realizes what a tiny fragile women Effie was. He's thankful her eyes are closed. He does not want to remember her death stare. Her face is dark blue and unnaturally swollen. Her blood-saturated ivory nightgown is pulled up almost to her waist and is unbuttoned, exposing one of her breasts. It pains him so much he can barely speak.

"Fix her . . .." He moves out of the way and motions Cheryl toward her side. "She wouldn't want to be seen like that. Fix her."

Cheryl pulls the gown together with trembling fingers, carefully buttons it, and smooths it down so her private area and legs are covered.

"There." Then Cheryl looks down at her bloody hands and, with a start, stares back up at Silas.

"Oh, Silas, no, we can't touch anything in here. We have to go in the other room."

"I'm staying with her." Someone has to until the ambulance comes, he thinks.

"We're contaminating a crime scene if we stay in this room."

Silas, still staring down at Effie, ignores her. His voice is a broken child's. "Look what they did to her."

"I know, but we have to let the police examine her. Come on." Cheryl gets him to his feet. She looks down one last time at the body, and glimpses something in Effie's frozen hand.

"What is that?" She leans down further. "Is that a piece of pantyhose?"

"What?" Silas stumbles against the bed. She steadies him.

"Doesn't matter. They'll find it," she tells him. His knees keep giving way as Cheryl struggles to guide him down the hall. She puts her arms around him, helping him to the kitchen sink. After pouring him a glass of water, she runs the tap over her hands, filling the sink with pinkish water.

Silas spots Effie's phone on the floor. It's unplugged but not cut. "Need to call the police."

Cheryl reconnects the phone to the wall socket and punches the programmed Police button. She puts it on speaker mode.

"Medicine Wheel Police Department." The voice belongs to Shelby Myers, Assistant Chief of Police, the newest hunk-in-uniform in the area. His move to Medicine Wheel from Deputy in Lawton had set local girls fluttering six months ago.

"Officer Myers, that you?" Her voice sounds shaky.

"Yes, how can I help you?"

"It's Cheryl Jackson out at the R.V. Village."

"What's the matter, Cheryl?"

"I'm at Effie Lawrence's place. Silas and I just found her." Cheryl's voice breaks. "She's dead."

There is a slight pause at the other end, then, "You mean, she's passed away?"

"No, someone's killed her. And the place is a mess."

"Don't touch anything, Cheryl. We're on our way."

Cheryl hangs up and helps Silas out onto the deck. His face is fish belly white by the time he slumps into a chair, almost gasping for breath. Neither of them speaks. He stares up into a deep turquoise sky, its beauty almost mocking. For a moment, he is back in Auschwitz, watching impossibly pink clouds drift above the stench of black smoke rising from the crematoriums. His fists tighten.

I never told her how much I loved her. Of all people, I should know about time.

Even though it's only minutes, it seems an eternity before Shelby Myers speeds toward them up Turquoise Drive, the

Medicine Wheel cruiser lit up in blue and red. By the time the Assistant Police Chief arrives, a few curious neighbors are already starting to gather across the street, near Silas's porch.

CHAPTER FOUR

Cheryl can already feel something important has ended. Just like that, Effie, sweet, religious zealot, and R.V. Village fixture, has been snatched away. And Cheryl hates herself for wanting a drink so bad.

Her heart pounds when she remembers she was next door in a drunken blackout when it happened. Dark, fleeting images stop Cheryl in her tracks: Doyle leaning over her in his cowboy hat, one hand around her breast, his breath smelling like chili and beer and breath mints.

Then, somehow, somebody was screaming for help. Is she really remembering this? Or was it a dream? Or Effie calling, begging for help, as someone slashed away at her?

Chief of Police Asa Bointy, a 55-year-old Kiowa Native, comes roaring in half an hour later from Lake Latonka, his weekend fishing trip with his Army buddies cut short. He is an inch from retirement and probably wishes he were already there after walking through Effie's place. He emerges, perspiring and shaking his head in disbelief.

"It's a bad one," he says in his soft-spoken Native lilt.

"You can say that again," Shelby agrees, but part of him seems to enjoy being the first officer on the scene. Getting thrown into a murder investigation undoubtedly beats his uneventful neighborhood rounds in their quiet, cobblestone town, Cheryl thinks.

Bointy forces his sagging girth into one of Effie's narrow porch chairs. "I called the Medical Examiner on my way in."

"Bet he didn't like that." Shelby chuckles. Off his boss's side glance, he looks down and paws the gravel with his boots. "I just meant on a Sunday and all."

"I thought I'd be cleaning catfish this morning, too," Bointy says. "So it goes." Directly descended from a great Kiowa war chief, his demeanor is imposing. He juggles the stub of a cigar from one side of his mouth to the other.

It is silent for a moment, as if no one knows where to begin. Then the Chief says, "Effie Lawrence, of all people." He glances at the growing crowd across the street around Silas's mobile home and then back at Shelby. "Best secure the area."

"Done, Sir." The Assistant Chief, in great shape for his forty years, is used to doing the moving and lifting for Bointy, whose uniforms now barely button over his belly.

Silas, fighting back emotion, tells the Chief, "I've seen plenty of death, but not . . . not like this."

Bointy nods his head. "Me neither, and I've been doing this a long time. She was an awful sweet lady. I know you cared about her, Mr. Weintraub. He studies Effie's wine-colored chrysanthemums for a moment. "An awful lot of overkill, wasn't it?"

"Some . . . animal," Cheryl whispers.

The growing crowd of neighbors keeps its distance across the street, but the Chief's presence has piqued everyone's curiosity. Bointy finally stands up and acknowledges them with a wave. "I might as well tell you the same way I got it, folks. Effie Lawrence is dead."

The gathering takes the news with shock and disbelief. Then they start to pepper him with questions. When was it, how did it happen, and why?

Bointy pushes his hands down to quell any discussion. "I can't say anything at all about it yet. We'll be talking to all of you, but for now, unless you saw or heard something last night, just go on to church or back to your homes. Please."

While they wait for the M.E. from Lawton, Chief Bointy, Assistant Chief Myers, Cheryl and Silas gather around in Effie's deck chairs.

"Cheryl, you're right next door. Did you hear anything?" Bointy asks.

She feels herself redden with guilt. A possible drunk dream is hardly a statement.

"I'd give anything if I had."

"Silas?"

"Nope. Last time I talked with her was about 9:30 last night when I was taking the horde out for their last potty of the night."

"Horde?" Myers asks.

"The dogs." Silas has four Chihuahuas who have him

thoroughly trained. "Anyway, I saw her out here, and we solved the problems of the world for a few minutes."

"How did she seem?" Bointy asks.

"Just fine. Pretty Boy Floyd is her favorite, and she was sweet talking him a bit. Said she was going straight to bed after the news. And, sorry to say, once I take my pills, I'm out for the count."

"Well, we'll talk to everybody. Although a lot of the folks in the Village couldn't hear a buffalo herd stampede right past their door." Asa nods at Shelby. "Have you checked the perimeter fence?"

"Not yet," Shelby says. "I was waiting for you to get here."

"Go ahead. I'll hold down the scene here."

Shelby nods and heads toward the large chain link fence that surrounds the R.V. park. The Chief turns his attention to Cheryl. "So, when did you last see her?"

It was yesterday afternoon, she tells him, when Cheryl swept and mopped Effie's deck for her. Effie worked outside on her immaculate lawn, enjoying the autumn sun, picking up the day's new collection of fallen leaves by hand.

Cheryl looks around at Effie's leaf-free yard and then remembers, "She was giving me grief about my messy yard. Well deserved, I admit it. And she was griping about her minister, which is par for the course."

Bointy glances at Cheryl's lawn then turns back to her and Silas. "They cut off some of her toes. Did you notice that?"

Silas' head jerks up. "They what?" He looks as though he might fall apart again.

Cheryl gasps and shakes her head. With so much blood everywhere, what had been done to Effie's feet apparently had not registered with either her or Silas.

"They wanted something from her real bad, to do all that to her before she was killed. You were close to her, Silas," Bointy continues. "You know of any enemies? Anything that happened recently?"

Silas squints through bloodshot eyes and shakes his head. "No, not really."

Cheryl can see from Silas's color that his blood sugar levels are low. It's almost 11:00, and he probably hasn't eaten a bite. Her own head is pounding, but that's no excuse to forget to remind him to eat. It's part of what she does every day. Still, it feels like she's somewhere else, where even the simplest tasks escape her.

"Do you mind if I get him something to eat, Chief?" Then she mouths aside, "Diabetes." Bointy nods an okay to her just as Shelby hurries across Effie's tiny backyard to the deck.

"Chief?" He looks excited. "Someone snipped through the fence." He gestures back toward an area of the chain link perimeter. "Looks like they got in that way."

The Chief stands and looks at it. "Better enlarge the crime scene then." Shelby gets the roll of yellow plastic ribbon and starts to work.

"When you finish that, why don't you go pick us up some

burgers?" Bointy tells him.

"You don't need me here?" The Assistant Chief looks disappointed. "Okay then. Red Barn okay?"

"I like Shorty's better," the Chief replies.

As Silas and Cheryl head across the street to Silas's, the Medical Examiner shows up with a crime scene technician in tow. Pink-cheeked and 30ish, the M.E. carries a leather bag and wears a sharp beige suit. He was probably heading to church when they found him.

Back at Silas's place, Cheryl settles him into his recliner with a glass of orange juice, starts a fresh pot of coffee, and warms up some chicken noodle soup she made last week. The juice settles his blood sugar.

She sips at a mug of coffee herself, watching the conference between the Police Chief and the M.E. from Silas's kitchen window. They speak too low for her to hear anything.

Silas abruptly asks, "What in hell was Doyle the Boil doing over at your place last night? I thought you hated him."

It feels like a punch to the gut. So, Doyle *was* at her place last night. Even given the scattered clothes leading into her bedroom, the confirmation still stuns her.

Instead of answering, Cheryl takes four Ibuprofen from Silas's bottle on the counter—thinking like an alcoholic. If two are prescribed, double that and you're golden. She ladles out their soup and puts it on the table, but Silas continues tapping his foot impatiently, not tolerating her avoidance of his question.

"Well?" he finally says.

"What?" But she sees his look. "You mean Doyle? At my place? You must be mistaken."

"Maybe you better think that through again." His laugh is dry and knowing.

That rankles her. Sometimes it's okay that Silas acts like her father, prying into her life as if she were ten years old. Not today.

"And maybe it's none of your business," Cheryl snaps. The moment it pops out, she's sorry. She's never been able to set boundaries, which is even harder in Medicine Wheel, where people seem to know what you're doing before you do it.

When pushed, like now, her response usually comes off as caustic. But she has always watched herself around Silas Weintraub. Since she came back to her hometown with her tail between her legs, he has been her nosy, adopted uncle across the street. It could be annoying, for sure, but right now she wants to kick herself.

"I'm sorry, Silas. That was . . . I'm so sorry," she stumbles. But he doesn't seem to be listening. She doesn't know whether it's typical male oblivion or Silas's gift for blowing off rebuffs.

The fact is, Silas is right. It galls her, but she knows deep down it is shame that kept her from telling Chief Bointy that Doyle was at her place last night, not just uncertainty about what happened between them. It is humiliating that she would ever turn to her worthless ex for comfort. As penance, she promises herself to find Doyle later today and ask him if he heard anything coming from Effie's place.

CHAPTER FIVE

After he returns from the hamburger run, Shelby Myers sees a large group of locals gathered across the street. He knows it is no use trying to shoo them away. This is too big an event in a largely drama-free town. Everyone is going to gawk.

At that moment a speeding BMW luxury sedan, its motor purring like a sleek cat, rushes toward them down Turquoise Lane. The milling onlookers perk up, realizing the first kin are arriving. And these are the kind of kin that people love to whisper about.

Even Shelby tries not to smile at the hastiness of their arrival. Just like them to rush here, now that the old lady's dead. Within a month after he moved to Medicine Wheel, the Assistant Chief had picked up on the gossip about the Lawrences. Running his fingers through his shiny dark hair, he bites off a quarter of his burger, and prepares to play gate keeper.

Katie Lawrence jumps out of the car first, forty-ish and as beautiful as a lot of money can make you. In a salmon-colored leather coat, flawless blonde streaks in a bouffant helmet, and, given the tightness of her skin, a serious attachment to BOTOX.

Sobbing, she hurries up the steps toward Effie's door. On her heels comes the actual blood relative, her husband Cliff, hair pomade, wearing a shiny gray suit, rings all over his manicured fingers. "Honey, calm down now."

Katie hurries toward Shelby so fast, he barely gets his hands up in a stop signal.

"You can't go in there, ma'am. M.E. is still working."

"That's my aunt," she screams at Shelby, who knows that's only technically true. It was Cliff's father who was a brother to Effie's long dead husband, Ben. Everyone in town knows Effie could barely stand the pair of them.

Cliff catches up with his wife and holds up the yellow Crime Scene ribbon himself for them to duck under. Shelby grabs the ribbon away from Cliff and repositions himself between them and Effie's front door."

"Doesn't matter who you are, sir. You're not allowed."

By this time Bointy has come to the door. "Sorry, Cliff, Katie," he says, stepping outside. "Official police business."

Cliff scoffs at their protocol. "Now you listen here. That's my aunt in there."

Shelby keeps his voice calm but firm. "Doesn't matter, it's a crime scene. Nobody gets in there."

Bointy nods in agreement, then moves Cliff and Katie to one side of the deck and speaks with them in hushed tones.

Across the street, Silas and Cheryl step outside to watch. "Yeah, now they show up," Silas sneers.

Cheryl lowers her voice. "And they'll wring this for every last drop." But no matter how much disdain the two of them throw at the entitled couple, it doesn't soften the blow.

An unexpected rain blows in, darkening the turquoise sky to deep indigo. The gawkers hurry under nearby porch overhangs. Falling leaves are grabbed midflight and pushed to the ground with the water's weight. Artillery booms from Ft. Sill split the sky with uncanny timing. Everybody jumps, as though they've been shot. Raindrops begin to splat like bb's on Effie's deck.

As Assistant Chief Myers tries to salvage the wet burgers from the deck table, Cliff and Katie see Cheryl and Silas on his porch and hurry over to take shelter with them. Cliff puts a protective arm around Katie, who is working herself up to a wail.

"Oh, she can't be gone, she just can't." Katie carefully pats away the mascara smears under her eyes.

"Oh, for God's sake," Silas mutters under his breath. Cheryl elbows him.

The four of them stand, without speaking, behind the sheet of rain pouring down from Silas's metal roof.

CHAPTER SIX

"I'm Cheryl, alcoholic." The words echo against the basement walls of the Medicine Wheel Christian Church as everyone introduces themselves. Tonight, the AA circle includes antsy newcomers, their legs pumping like pneumatic drills, a professionally dressed woman, a couple of biker dudes in black leather jackets, and Natives with long braids.

One of the Natives, Gus Tippiconnie, is a close friend of Asa Bointy's and part of a trio of Native Vietnam vets who breakfast together regularly. Cheryl is used to seeing Gus at meetings and nods when their eyes meet.

One of the bikers, Lex, a recovering meth head Cheryl has seen a few times before, leads the meeting. Before he calls on Cheryl, he shares how lost he was until he figured out his "har par."

She glances around to see if anyone got what he said.

"Nobody could tell me nothing," Lex says. "I'd look around at you guys and think, why do I gotta come here? I'm nothing like y'all." Then he grins around at the circle. "Except for the fact I wanted to be high every minute of the day. Other than that, we got nothing in common."

Everyone chuckles knowingly.

"So whether your 'har par' is your bike, or a spirit or God

. . .."

His words fade as Cheryl realizes he's butchering "higher power" as only an Okie could. She finds it endearing.

When Lex finishes, he looks at Cheryl. "How about you?"

This is the last thing she wants. Most of them here know she came regularly to meetings and then abruptly stopped a few months ago. Lex coaxes her. "Cheryl, would you like to share?"

She sighs. No, not really, she thinks. But when you're called on, you say something. That's sort of the rule.

"I'm Cheryl, alcoholic."

"Hi, Cheryl," the group responds.

"I've been struggling, kind of lost, really. Trying to get back to meetings for a long time, it seems like. It's been a tough few weeks, and I really don't have that many friends to talk to about it. The old ones are still hanging out drinking, and I don't dare go around bars, anyway. Drunks like me can't do that. They say if you hang around a beauty shop long enough, sooner or later you're going to get your bleached.

Warm laughter around the circle. This is an analogy they've heard before. "At least I have a desire not to drink tonight. I think I need to listen."

"Glad you're here," Lex adds, echoed by others in the group.

Cheryl listens for the next hour to addicts sharing their experiences and hope with each other. She wants to feel close to them, but it's just not there. They're on the wagon and she's not. Not that she needs to be dry to attend, but by not being able to show up sober, she must acknowledge that the long, insidious arms of the disease have lulled her in again.

After the meeting, she's surprised to find Gus waiting for her outside. He nods a hello. "Sorry to hear about Miss Lawrence."

"Yeah," she says. "It doesn't feel real yet."

"Yep," Gus nods. "She was . . . kind to my family."

Cheryl looks at his prematurely white hair, worn flannel shirt and jeans—one of the most unassuming people she's ever met. Other than facing the world with his head up, there is no other hint of the decorated warrior from Vietnam, who served bravely and then had to soldier on as a P.O.W. in Hanoi for two more years. His face is etched with crags that should belong to a face ten years older.

Cheryl surprises herself by blurting out. "What an awful way to die." Then she is crying. Saying it out loud makes her crumble.

Gus pats her shoulder and hoods his eyes for a few moments. "When she was an Indian nurse, Miss Effie would come out and take care of my uncle. He had psoriasis, awful bad. Nobody in the family wanted to touch him, really, the way his skin flaked off everywhere, and how he scratched at himself something awful. But Miss Effie, she'd come out and wash him with cool rags and rub baby oil on him. I was always grateful for her. I sure would like to know who did it." Something dark in his tone surprises her. She leans back and notices his jaw jutting forward a little.

"I'd give anything, too," she agrees.

"Well, Asa will be on top of it." Gus studies her for a moment. "You let me know if there's anything I can do for you."

"Thank you." Cheryl wraps him in a spontaneous hug. "I mean it."

Somewhere between that warm hug and when she is sitting once again behind the wheel of her pickup, Cheryl gets lost again. She feels so lonely and spent. She checks her watch. Fifteen minutes before the liquor store closes. She hates herself for it, but she decides she can't face Effie's funeral tomorrow without a drink.

After she gets home and downs the first drink, though, she has to wonder if maybe the meeting did a little good. It just doesn't taste as great as she expected it would.

CHAPTER SEVEN

Police Chief Asa Bointy stands on the steps of Medicine Wheel Methodist Church, watching over the crowd assembled to say goodbye to Effie Lawrence. Just yesterday his new uniforms, which he had been forced to order in yet another larger size, finally arrived. What they cost kills him, but at least he won't have to go around the next two months sucking in his gut so his undershirt doesn't bulge through the buttonholes.

Funerals in Medicine Wheel are both a parting ritual and a social affair. The retirees are always genuinely torn up to lose another of their dwindling community, but also grateful it isn't them going to push up daisies. So, although it takes place under blanketing gray skies, the affair is talkative, even gossipy.

People who don't get out that often come to say goodbye and check out younger relatives, discussing in hushed tones whether the next generation is a perennial embarrassment to the deceased or passes muster with the family.

Enemies and friends alike show up, though keenly aware of their proximity to one another. People who despise each other can somehow manage to stand only a few feet apart yet avoid speaking to one another all day long.

In Effie's case, her friends abound, her reputation tarnished only by what's left of her family—her nephew and his wife—although this will remain unspoken today. Cliff owns the local John Deere franchise, which is impressive, but he ruined his social standing in Medicine Wheel when he shotgun-married Katie Jones, the daughter of local moonshiners.

Once everyone is inside the small sanctuary, which overflows with flowers, the service begins. Katie and Cliff both sit in the front pew, and despite her grief, she wears neon blue for the occasion, with a matching wide-brimmed hat that won't last ten seconds in the Oklahoma wind.

No one dislikes the pretentious rich quite like a small town. Too many locals remember Katie as the cheerful slut she was in high school, voted Outstanding Receiver by the Tornadoes, Medicine Wheel's football team. And most people liked her better that way than this Katie, constantly striving to rewrite her history.

As it happened, Katie's "pregnancy" had turned out to be a hysterical one. "Oops," she had said, but they stayed together anyway, and Cliff glad-handed his way back up to V.I.P. status in Medicine Wheel. Still, nobody is dying to have coffee with them down at the Big Chief Diner, either.

Bointy knows the Jones family's moonshining has segued over the years to cooking meth. Luckily, he has never been tasked to confirm it, since he would probably get himself shot to pieces in the process. Meth is a nasty business, but the local cooks were like bootleggers before liquor was legal . . . better to stick with the devil you know sometimes. At least they don't blow up their own labs or shoot at cattle for something to do on Saturday night.

Silas sits stoically beside Cheryl, eyes downcast, his jaw as clenched as a bear trap. In the two weeks since Effie's death he has barely eaten and has sunk into a depression that flares up as barely controlled anger.

The loquacious minister did not take the time to craft a short elegy, and the congregation is coughing and rustling. If not on everybody's lips, murder is still on everyone's mind, but this is left completely unaddressed by the talky preacher.

It is amazing how they have fixed Effie up for the traditional viewing. The blue-black bruises, the painful swelling, the cuts and blood, have disappeared under the pale, waxy semblance of who she was.

After the elegy, Cliff and Katie, her last remaining family, stand by the casket, greeting everyone in a receiving line. When Silas and Cheryl reach the front of the line, it quickly becomes apparent Silas has not backed off an inch from his loathing of Effie's relatives. After standing a long time looking at Effie in the casket, he turns and heads in the opposite direction of the receiving line.

"Silas?" Cheryl whispers, "did you want to . . ..?" She glances toward Cliff and Katie.

He frowns and speaks low. "Not going to talk to them. Let's go." Then he raises his voice for a parting shot. "I can't stand either one of them." Everyone within earshot freezes for a moment. It is not a mortal sin to dislike people in small towns, but one never announces it in public.

Heading to the graveside interment, Cheryl is grateful Silas agreed to bring his wheelchair for this last leg. She's concerned about his staying on his feet much longer. Plus, he's so prickly she wants to be able to roll him away quickly if he turns combative.

By the time they make it to the cemetery, a twenty mile-an-hour wind is flapping the awning over the grave site. It blows without mercy at the huddled comb-overs and bangs carefully arranged to hide receding hairlines. After everyone's flowers are atop the casket, Silas drops a single yellow rose. As the casket creaks down into the earth, people drift back to their cars.

As Cheryl and Silas are getting into her pickup to leave, she looks up to see Cliff Lawrence hurrying toward them.

"You want to tell me why both of you have been called in for the legalities tomorrow?" Cliff speaks low but doesn't keep the anger out of his voice.

"What are you talking about?" she asks. Actually, Darwin Smith, Effie's ancient lawyer *did* ask her and Silas to come to the bank the next morning on some legal matters, but Cheryl assumed it was because she knows where most of Effie's papers are.

Silas, annoyed that he can't quite hear them from inside the cab, slaps the side of the pickup door. "Gotta go, Cheryl. For the love of God, I'm getting sick. Come on."

Shaking, Cheryl climbs in the pickup. Silas pats her arm as she composes herself.

"So much for their mourning period, huh?" she manages to quip. Then she realizes Silas is chuckling.

"They know. Ha." He slaps his knee.

That barely registers. As the shock of the confrontation begins to wear off, her own indignation takes its place.

"What did she mean, anyway? Plenty of people leave

some little something for nurses or care givers in their will. What is the big deal?"

"I bet Effie stuck it to 'em. They thought she was their doormat." He bends down to look up through the windshield at the sky. "Good goin,' girl. Yep, look who's smilin' now."

He scratches up a laugh. She smiles through her confusion, but Cheryl's stomach feels like something is clawing at it from the inside.

CHAPTER EIGHT

The next morning, Silas Weintraub is almost rubbing his hands with glee over what he knows is coming, but he won't feel relieved until it is formalized. The office in Pioneer Bank is a bit cramped for the reading of Effie Lawrence's will. The four attendees—Cheryl, Silas, Cliff, Katie—exchange terse greetings as they arrive almost simultaneously.

Silas and Cheryl go for the two chairs across from the desk where Darwin Smith is seated, leaving a small love seat for the Lawrences. Silas doesn't want to sit any closer to Katie than necessary. Her heavy patchouli scent brings tears to his eyes. He'd rather inhale diesel fumes.

In addition to Katie's scent, the air in the office seems charged with loathing, and a fleeting nervous body odor. A bank officer delivers Effie's security box then sinks into a corner chair to document the meeting.

Darwin tries for a game face, but he looks like someone preparing to withstand a flogging. "Now, technically, Mrs. Effie Lawrence died intestate, without a Last Will and Testament."

Cliff relaxes a little back into his seat. "We figured as much." He and Katie exchange smug little smiles. "In which case, her estate automatically reverts to family survivors."

"Normally, yes," Smith says, cringing slightly, as though waiting for the first whiplash. "Except Mrs. Lawrence informed me recently that she had left a notarized letter in her security box, indicating that she intended it to serve as her will."

No one says anything, but Cliff's crunched forehead indicates he's been caught flat footed. "Is that even legal?"

"The court will have to rule, of course, but it is a holographic will, written in her hand, and does show intent. So, shall I read the letter aloud?" Smith looks around and everyone nods.

"To Whom It May Concern: I, Effie Lawrence, being of sound mind and a hospital-free body, leave this document as my Last Testament of what should be done with my estate in the event of my death."

"You're kidding." Katie gives an unbelieving giggle. Cliff puts a hand on her knee and sits forward.

Silas is not surprised that both are suddenly vigilant. If Effie did what she intended, it would be a kick in the butt for them. Effie didn't like that Cliff and Katie nosed around about her assets and discovered the sizable portfolio Effie had grown over the years. In fact, their remodel of the cabin, which they bought from Effie, started soon after. Effie was irked by the couple's assumption that a substantial inheritance was heading their way.

Smith shuffles his reading glasses back and forth on his nose as he continues.

"I leave this world with all debts paid in full. I have no outstanding loans or credit card debt, and my funeral arrangements have been prepaid. Therefore, I leave $10,000 to Medicine Wheel Methodist Church, to be used exclusively for poverty programs and to send needy children to summer camps, and not one penny on more fancy statues and stained-glass windows. And tell that preacher I mean business."

Silas chuckles. Effie bitched about her long-time minister for years, saying he had turned into a pompous sycophant who stopped listening to his older congregation. Silas had helped sweet little Effie plan how to exact her revenge.

Smith clears his throat and moves on. "As to my remaining estate, I leave it all to someone who has lovingly cared for me during my twilight years."

Cliff and Katie hunch forward, looking grateful to get to the part that counts. But Silas, who has forced himself to stay uncharacteristically quiet, sits back, grinning at Cheryl, who looks like she's still trying to figure out why she is here.

Above the lawyer's lips tiny perspiration beads form. "I wish that Cheryl Lee Jackson receive all moneys, property, and her red pickup, which, if it is not paid for when I die, it is to be paid off immediately with moneys from the estate."

Cliff and Katie both look like they've been bitch-slapped. Katie gives out a little cry.

The reading goes on. "I want you all to take this seriously, as I have no intention of paying my lawyer several thousand dollars just to write down what I can say in these few sentences."

Darwin glances up at everyone and tries to inject a shrugging little smile into the proceedings. Seeing this is unappreciated, he clears his throat and moves on.

"If anybody in my family should try to contest or thwart this document, I give Silas Weintraub, my dear friend and neighbor, full authority to initiate and pursue every legal remedy known to man against them. These are my last wishes, that my chosen family, rather than my bloodline, be recognized as the dearest people to me on this earth."

The lawyer removes his glasses and tells them, "It's signed by Effie Lawrence."

Even though Cheryl looks numb, her eyes are moist with emotion. When she finally glances at Cliff and Katie, they are both glaring at the lawyer.

Cliff's voice is an icy growl. "What's the date on that?"

Smith, now sweating profusely, looks at the bottom of the document. "It was signed and notarized by a bank officer on April 6th of this year."

Katie puffs up and points a manicured finger at Silas. "This is that little Jew's work."

Though stunned by her remark, Silas manages to push out his lips in a self-satisfied smirk and chuckles.

Cliff, politically sharper than his wife, puts a quick hand on her arm. "Now, honey, let's don't say anything we'll regret."

It looks as though Katie is about to defend her slur, but he squeezes her arm firmly. Then they turn to Cheryl, who sits there in dry-mouthed astonishment.

Effie never dropped her a single hint about any of this. And, as far as Cheryl knows, Effie's estate is probably quite modest. Silas, however, understands why Cliff and Katie are looking at Cheryl as if she's absconded with the family jewels. Because, without knowing it, she has.

As soon as a clean exit is possible, the Lawrences whisk

out with mumbled goodbyes, leaving the rest of them still in their chairs. Cheryl seems barely able to focus as the lawyer goes over the upcoming legal calendar. There is plenty of filing and adjudicating ahead, and he will be in touch, he says, when the wheels are in motion.

During the drive back to the R.V. Village in the pickup, Cheryl seems oddly shut down. But Silas chatters like a magpie.

"And the look on Katie's face. Yeah, this little Jew did his work, alright. They'll never see a penny of . . .."

"Silas," Cheryl interrupts. "How big a deal is this? I mean, after the church and this pickup get paid off, I can't imagine there'll be much else left."

He grins and winks at her. "We'll see."

She shrugs. "Well, if I can top off my propane tank for the winter, I'll be happy."

"Just as long as you don't use it to buy booze."

Cheryl closes her eyes, looking humiliated that he said it, yet mildly annoyed by his naivete. "Silas, when you're an alcoholic, no matter how down and out you are, you can always find something to drink. Money just means you get to go to hell with the high shelf whiskey instead of no label vodka."

For once, he lets her have the last word.

CHAPTER NINE

On Thursday, four days after the funeral, Cheryl sits atop the steps to her deck and watches the sunrise over the Wichita Mountains. She finally gave up on getting back to sleep at five a.m. and put on coffee.

Now, the night sky grudgingly gives way to a peach-colored sun that cuts through the range's purple shadows.

She savors the light morning buzz of insects, the damp smell of cedar, and a bracing cup of dark coffee. Sitting out like this, soaking up nature, still supplies her best connection to a higher power.

Cheryl has never had the same clarity about her gods as Effie. But she knows when she hit bottom and asked whatever powers that be for help, she had—and this is still miraculous to her—somehow stopped drinking. A force she still can't describe or understand carried her through. Even though her head feels too muddled to meditate, that's what she wants again.

Her work has taken on a sudden head of steam. Grateful for the income, she knows a lot of it comes from nosing around for inside information from the person who found Effie, especially since no one's been arrested yet. Still, she's happy to be taking three clients to shop for groceries today, plus chauffeuring the Boney sisters to and from Bingo at the Buffalo Thunder Casino, and multiple taxi service errands to doctors and rest homes.

The hectic schedule is working. Cheryl only had two drinks last night, falling asleep from sheer exhaustion.

The shock of Effie's death is beginning to wear off, leaving an aching sense of loss. She would give anything to sit with her neighbor again, the way they used to "take the morning air," as Effie called it, watching the birds and talking of local news and gossip.

She goes inside, takes her shower and throws her clothes on. As she's walking out the door a little before eight, her phone rings. Probably one of the day's clients. She gives her official greeting. "Cheryl's Personal Services."

"Cheryl? Chief Bointy here."

She's surprised he's at work this early. "Hey Chief. What's up?"

"Couple of things I'd like to go over with you . . . just clearing up some details. Need you to come down to the station."

It takes her by surprise. "I'd be glad to, but I'm pretty much slammed all day."

There is a slight wait, then Asa's tone sounds more businesslike. "Maybe you could rearrange some things?"

"Has something happened?" She tries mentally to fit adding a police station visit to an already daunting schedule.

"We'll talk when you get down here."

The sudden disruption of her day still doesn't sink in. "So, any time today?"

After a pause, he says, "I was thinking the sooner the better. Like, now?"

Something should click, Cheryl senses, but it doesn't. "Okay, I'll figure it out." She looks at her list, makes phone calls, assuring everyone she's just running late and will get back to them.

She limps into the Police station at 8:30. Inside it smells like stale cigarette smoke, collected over decades. It reminds her of week-old body odor. Everybody knows the new NO SMOKING sign is merely a nod to the City Council. In Oklahoma, where a third of its citizens still light up and cowboy rules large apply, the policing of even toxic habits is considered an impudent intrusion—just one more gateway for the government to take over the world. Prevailing thought is that people ought to be allowed to kill themselves in the manner they prefer.

The Chief seats her on the other side of his desk, while Shelby Myers hovers across the aisle, standing by his cubicle. She notices he has the department's one computer set up in his area and can't help but wonder if the Chief even knows how to turn one on.

Bointy starts. "Now, Cheryl, before we get started, I'm required by law to tell you that you do have the right to remain silent, and that anything you can be used against--"

"Uh, 'can and will,' Chief," Shelby throws in.

"What?" Bointy's eyebrows squeeze together.

"Any you say can *and will* be used against you in a court of law, Chief."

Cheryl can't believe what they're saying. "Are you Mirandizing me?"

"It's for all our protection," the chief continues. "You have the right to an attorney. If you don't have an attorney, one will be provided for you."

She still can't wrap her head around this. "Am I a . . . why am I here?"

"We just have a few more questions for you, Cheryl," Bointy says.

Shelby adds, "You can waive your right to an attorney. These are technical warnings that we're required to give before interviews."

"So I'm not a suspect?"

"No," Bointy says with a shake of his head.

"Well, I don't have anything to hide," Cheryl says. "It's just . . . why would I need an attorney?"

"I don't know." Bointy shifts in his chair toward her. "But we have to ask. You know. If you think you need one."

"What I need is to get to work," Cheryl says.

Shelby leans in slightly. "Like he said, you can always waive the attorney thing, and we can get right to it."

"Yeah," Cheryl nods, "I haven't done anything wrong."

"Fine," Bointy says and begins with routine questions. He takes her through everything again, step-by-step of her actions that awful morning. Today, he seems particularly interested in where and how she touched Effie's body.

"Now when you fixed Effie's gown, how did . . . what did you actually do?"

Cheryl uses her hands to demonstrate. "I just pulled it down—it was bunched up over her stomach—so her private areas were exposed. I put it back in place," she says, spontaneously remembering Silas's painful grimace at seeing Effie that way.

"Why do you think the gown was raised up over her hips?" he asks.

Her voice sounds unsteady. "I didn't know. It did flash through my mind that maybe someone had . . . I don't know, maybe raped her."

Both men stare at her. "Or wanted to make it look that way, maybe?" Bointy suggests.

"Like I said, I don't know. But Silas was upset to see her like that. He asked me to fix her gown, so I did."

The chief opens a file and reads from earlier notes. "You said when you first saw her, one of her breasts was exposed as well."

"Right. Silas and me felt, well, I guess, humiliated for her. Wouldn't anyone have wanted to cover her? What are you getting at?"

Bointy pencils something in a margin.

Out of the blue, Cheryl recalls the little piece of hosiery gripped in Effie's hand. She tries to remember if she told them about it. "Did they find—I don't know if I mentioned this before—a scrap of, like, pantyhose in one of her hands?"

"Pantyhose?" Bointy asks.

"Yes, gripped in her hand. I thought maybe she had ripped it away . . . you know, like some kind of pantyhose mask?" She feels a nervous dampness in her arm pits.

"Oh, yeah." The chief looks at Shelby, who nods.

"Yesh, the crime techies took it. The tests on it aren't back yet." Shelby turns to a file in his hand labeled *Cheryl Jackson*. "So, let's go over your relationship with Miss Lawrence. How you knew her and so forth."

"Okay," Cheryl says and glances at her watch. "When I moved back home a few years ago, I moved in next door to Effie." Shelby frowns at something in the file. "That was soon after the charge in Oklahoma County?"

She grimaces. As if he doesn't already know all that. Is he going to go back through, blow by blow? "Six months after, yes," she finally confirms.

Frowning, Shelby flips through some pages. "I'm not finding . . . that was for . . . ."

Bointy clears his throat. "A DUI." He looks a bit surprised by this line of questioning.

Undeterred, Shelby grunts as he finds the report. "Actually, Reckless Endangerment as well, wasn't it?"

CHAPTER TEN

The words hit her like a sonic boom. Panic. Shame. Guilt. Jabbing it at her so quickly, with no warning, starts her trembling. Everything comes pounding back.

Driving home drunk from happy hour, singing along to a Moby song, then from nowhere, darting out in front of her, two girls, laughing, paying no attention, racing on their bicycles . . . Cheryl slamming the brakes, somehow swerving away from them, the car speeding onto the shoulder, too fast, crazy fast, careening into blackness.

Her pale skin gets the chief's attention, apparently. Before Shelby can continue, Bointy jumps in. "Our department has been supervising Miss Jackson's parole since her return. I don't think we need to dwell on that."

Cheryl looks down at the floor, trying not to let anything show.

Shelby surprises her then. "I'm sorry. Didn't mean to upset you."

She wonders if that's true. Cheryl senses a certain relish in him, but realizes he's only been here six months. Still trying to make his bones. He wasn't around when Medicine Wheel's defeated basketball All-Star limped, literally, back into town, the only good news being that the bicycling girls weren't hurt. The DUI, the accident, her nearly ruined leg were on everyone's lips for months.

Let it go. Let it go and take a deep breath. She wipes her sweaty palms on her jeans. "It happened and it's over." Cheryl glances at the chief. "Well, almost."

Bointy nods and gently smiles. Two more months and you're a free woman."

"Oh," Shelby says, noting another report. "I see. Parole's up in December. Great. Good for you." When her response is a closed mouth smile, he picks up where he left off.

"So, you moved in next to Effie. But that wasn't the first time you met her, was it?"

"Oh, no, I grew up here, and it's a little town, so I've always known who she was. When I was a teenager, I remember her working as . . . what did they call them? Field nurses, I think it was, with different tribes in the area."

"Oh?" Shelby seems surprised.

"I remember the Kiowa called her Scissortail Woman. She got a kick out of that." Cheryl smiles at Chief Bointy, who nods in recognition.

Shelby looks confused. "That's the first I've heard that nickname. What did it mean? That she was a little thing who flew in and helped?"

Bointy leans forward. "She gave my gram her insulin shots and tried to get her to eat right. Not that it did much good . . . the healthy diet part, I mean."

"I didn't catch the traveling nurse thing." Shelby flushes. "Missed that somehow. She's been hard to track down professionally. It wasn't until I found her Army records where she was a nurse during the war that I got somewhere."

"Indian Affairs . . . yeah, they probably don't have their old records computerized yet." Bointy shrugs. "And I never thought to mention it."

"So, anyway," Shelby presses her, "you knew her growing up. And how'd you get started doing this working for old folks deal?"

Why is this guy always right on the edge of needling me? They're senior citizens of retirees, you idiot. Not that he seems to distinguish nuances.

"My personal services, you mean?" Cheryl dials back her attitude and goes on. "When I moved back from the city, I was not in a good place, and Effie realized I needed work. She asks me one day if I might be able to help a neighbor of hers who has Parkinson's It was just a part time thing, but before I knew it, word spread. It turns out lots of retirees need help with cooking, cleaning, running errands. Whatever."

"We got us a big retirement community, alright. Anybody else ever leave you money in their will?" Shelby asks.

"Couple of hundred once. Nothing big." Cheryl doesn't add that several passed on still owing her money, too, none of which she ever saw.

"The bank tells us Miss Lawrence bought you that new pickup of yours." Now back in his area of knowledge, Shelby sits back, waiting for her to explain.

"Effie didn't buy it, okay? She cosigned the note. My old Nissan bit the dust and I needed transportation to keep working, but--"

He interrupts her. "The old lady covered your last two payments, according to the bank."

Cheryl snaps at him. "Don't refer to her that way."

Shelby's eyes pop in surprise, but he quickly puts up his palms in apology. "No disrespect intended." After a moment. "But I still need you to answer the question."

"I was going through a hard spell with my finances. Three clients had died within a couple of months of each other. It was Effie's idea to help me out."

"When did you find out how much she was worth?" Another zinger.

"I have no idea what she's worth." Cheryl is ready to pop this guy if he doesn't back off.

Bointy clears his throat and gives Shelby a cautioning glance. It would seem his assistant chief's interview style is harsher than Bointy prefers.

Shelby acquiesces by switching directions. "Now you said you got home at what time on the night of the murder?"

"Since I'm not sure, I probably said I wasn't sure. I'd guess about one in the morning. Maybe later."

The chief puts his hand up to show he wants the next question. He leans in and studies Cheryl for a moment. "How come didn't you mention Doyle Lowe was with you?"

Cheryl pulls her head into the cowl of her sweater, like a

turtle sinking into its shell. So, they do know. Did you really think they wouldn't find out? That it wouldn't matter, you idiot.

"I don't know why I didn't mention it," she manages. They wait for more. "I really don't know." But it was certainly more than just Doyle. The truth is she knows full well that drinking violates her parole. Mentioning Doyle, or the hotel bar . . . or even having one drink. "I'm sorry," she finishes limply.

"What time did Doyle leave?" Shelby asks. "Or did he leave?"

He's just pissing me off now . . . with that eager beaver tone, his slick hair loaded with product. She stuffs it down. "I don't remember."

He doesn't let up. "Because Doyle says he left your place around 2:00, and he didn't hear anything from Miss Lawrence's place before then."

"Okay," she says. And makes herself stop there.

Shelby's eyes have a tease about them, as though there's something there that she isn't getting. She stays quiet, not about to play into whatever it is.

"How far away is your mobile home from the Lawrence place?" he goes on.

"Maybe twenty feet?"

"And since her mobile home is at the end of Turquoise Lane, and she has no neighbors on the other side, you would be the closest one." When she doesn't answer, he asks, "And it's your statement that you heard nothing from Miss Lawrence's place after Mr. Lowe left your house?"

"Right." Cheryl glances at Bointy as if to ask, "Are you seeing what he's doing here?"

Shelby's in a groove now. "Yet considering what was done to her, she had to be screaming for help."

Cheryl can't trust herself to speak. She knows she might start bawling.

It's silent for a few moments. Then Chief Bointy holds up an 8 X 10 manila envelope and waves it in the air. "We got evidence back from the lab. That's the main reason we called you in, Cheryl. There are a few fingerprints we've been able to identify."

Standing beside Bointy, Shelby looks self-satisfied. In fact, she suspects he's trying to hide a smirk. T

The light starts to dawn. "Well, I imagine you found mine, for sure." Cheryl stumbles, still trying to find her voice. "I was there when we found her. Plus, I was over there all the time."

Bointy says, "First, there is a bloody palm print from the dresser which belongs to you. And your fingerprints were on her gown. Bloody fingerprints."

It takes a moment to understand what he is saying. Then she remembers. "She--her breast—her breast was showing, like I told you. She was a modest woman. I . . . I fixed and buttoned the gown for her. She wouldn't have wanted to be seen like that. Ask Silas."

Cheryl realizes now that both men have detached expressions, curious but unconvinced. She can feel drops of perspiration fall onto her neck. From the army base, distant artillery maneuvers echo in the air.

For a moment, it's as though she is watching from somewhere way above the room: Two uniformed lawmen closing in on a woman who looks like her . . . fear, panic crashing in. Heart erupting. When she finally stops shaking, gets her bearings and looks up at the men, they are studying her like a specimen thumb tacked to the wall.

As Bointy gets up, his chair legs screech against the concrete. He leans over the table and says, not without pity in his voice, "I want to believe you, Cheryl. I really do. But there's no forced entry here. Nobody else's prints. Yours are all over that bedroom. And I got to tell you, not mentioning about your ex-husband being there?

We have to wonder what else you're leaving out. Like if you knew about Effie's will and wanted to hurry that along . . . well, it's a lot of coincidences. Can you see where I'm going with this?"

Cheryl reels as she sees how it all might look. "Leaving Doyle out, that was all. It was stupid of me, but I told you the truth about everything else."

Both lawmen look stoic, noncommittal.

Cheryl thinks about how crazy this is turning, how clients are waiting for her, for heaven's sake, how she needs to nip this in the bud. The thought of another personal scandal is beyond hideous. "Please just tell me what to do. There must be something I can do."

Shelby Myers studies her, then, almost nonchalantly,

turns to his boss. "Well, Chief, what if she took a polygraph?"

CHAPTER ELEVEN

Several hours later Cheryl remembers the warning that she could have asked for a lawyer. Anybody who has ever seen *Law and Order* knows, don't say anything, don't do anything without a lawyer. But earlier, it was something akin to a panic attack that made her agree to the polygraph.

She found herself bowing to a fearful harangue in her head, that insists she must make the accusation go away fast, must find an immediate remedy for the pressure. Instead of letting herself step back from the situation, she obsesses, instead, on what people will think. Her clients who count on her daily, Silas and how he will view it. The horror when it gets out. Collectively, it obliterates her last shred of sense.

Something in Cheryl cannot walk out of that station under suspicion. When she returned in shame to Medicine Wheel three years ago, she promised herself, *no more trouble with the law.* Then this morning, she told herself she was innocent and that was just what would show up on the test. Too humiliated to call anybody for advice, Cheryl sat and shook for an hour while a technician drove from Lawton to administer the polygraph.

Now, as Herb, the kindly, ancient polygraph technician, fits her up with the sensors, Cheryl assures herself this is the best, quick out. A polygraph may not be admissible in court, but it will get Asa and his ambitious assistant off her back. Even as her entire body races, she tells herself that the truth will set her free, literally. This mess that descended on her before the day even got going will be over by noon.

"Now, I'm going to ask you a couple of base line questions first, to get a reading and then there will be just a few others. Okay?" Herb explains.

"Right," Cheryl responds, looking around at the chipped paint on the interview room walls. They had moved in there so it would just be the two of them, although she's sure Bointy and Shelby are watching from the adjoining room.

"There's no need to be nervous. This machine doesn't magically say whether you're telling the truth or not, but you look like a smart girl, so I'm sure you knew that. It just records your anxiety levels, so just relax, take your time, and only answer yes or no."

She nods. He really does seem like a gentle man.

"Okay. We're going to start now. Is your name Cheryl Lee Jackson?" She's so unused to hearing her full name, it gives her a start.

"Yes, it is."

"Just yes or no, please."

"Yes."

"Wait. Let's start again." A moment goes by. "Is your name Cheryl Lee Jackson?"

"Yes."

"Is George H. Bush the President of the United States?"

"Yes." Herb is sitting behind her, and Cheryl can hear rustling papers. She figures he is moving on to the questions Chief Bointy wrote out for him to ask. But he surprises her.

"Is your mother's name Lois Ann Jackson?"

Hearing her name out of the blue stuns her. Could he have any idea what a trigger her mom is for her? It's as if her heart fumbles, remembering her mother's silent but palpable scorn after Cheryl returned home from the career-ending DUI in the city. It had nearly done her in.

It was her mother, not her father, who decided her parents wanted nothing more to do with her. And Cheryl had believed she deserved it, humiliating them the way she had. It was the metallic tone in her mother's voice that still stung, when she had said to Cheryl, "*Sorry* just doesn't cut it anymore, Cheryl Lee. You're no daughter of mine."

Herb clears his throat. "Miss Jackson?"

"Sorry."

"It's okay. One more time. Is your mother's name Lois Anne Jackson?"

Cheryl takes a deep breath and says, "Yes."

A pause. "Did you kill Effie Lawrence?"

"No." But her body feels like something has clutched it and tightening its grip.

"Do you know who did kill Effie Lawrence?"

"No."

"Do you have any knowledge regarding the murder of Effie Lawrence?"

Her heart drums against her ribs. "No."

A long moment. "Is there anything else you know about the murder of Effie Lawrence that you haven't told the police yet?"

Again, she says, "No."

Then it's over. Herb asks her to wait outside while he talks to Chief Bointy, and then they will let her know the results.

Shaky and dry-mouthed, she fishes around in her jeans for enough quarters to get a Diet Dr. Pepper out of the vending machine near the entrance.

She gulps it as she studies the Outstanding Warrant notices on a nearby board, some of them people she knows, or knows of. There of lots charges of DUI's, driving without a license, and no car insurance. In this area, lots of people still just take their chances.

"Jug" McMillan, a face from the past, jumps out at her from the board. The brutish drunk nearly stomped his wife to death before starting on the children, somehow made bail by putting up his shack of a house, then was a no show for his hearing. No one has seen "Jug" since, even though relatives, at least the ones who speak of him, say he is still hiding out in the area.

And "Jug" is not the only mystery. Two partial skeletal remains were discovered last year in the Wildlife Refuge, unearthed when some starving coyotes dragged them to the surface long after their deaths. Both were Ft. Sill soldiers, accused of brutally raping a local girl. It turned out Medicine Wheel didn't have jurisdiction, and the Army drug their feet on pressing charges. The party boys were last seen leaving a roadside bar, and never sighted again. Until the coyotes got to them.

Cheryl vaguely recalls that an anonymous donation helped the poor McMillan family get another little house somewhere. She's trying to recall the details when they call her back to the interview room. The way Chief Bointy avoids her eyes, Cheryl knows it can't be good.

When they're all seated, Bointy looks up at her and says, "The findings are 'Inconclusive.'"

She blinks in disbelief.

He goes on. "Now that's not the same thing as saying you were flat out deceptive. But it means there's something you're not telling us."

A heaviness drops into Cheryl's stomach, a dead weight that takes everything she has with it. It's an effort to speak.

"But I didn't kill Effie. Why else would I offer to take the . . . I should have asked . . . ." She realizes for the first time that she can't take care of this herself, that no matter how much she wills it to go away, it isn't about to. "What happens now?"

Bointy rubs his hands and stares at the floor. Shelby, quiet up to then, speaks softly to his boss, as though she isn't present. "If it was anybody else, somebody you didn't now, what would you do?" Then, although still speaking to Bointy, he turns toward Cheryl. "If we were in Lawton, I know what they'd do."

Chief Bointy nods somberly, like a man caught in a web, and looks across the table at her. "Sorry, Cheryl, but I'm going to have to hold you."

Everything except her own disbelief refuses to function. "You mean . . . arrest me? For what?"

"For right now, Obstruction of Justice."

CHAPTER TWELVE

After a stunned silence, Shelby asks, "Should I take her back?" Cheryl assumes he means to one of the two jail cells.

The Chief puts a hand up to stop him, then tells her, "You do have a phone calls."

Silas is the only person she can think of. He is the closest thing she's got to family here since Effie's gone. Reluctantly, she calls him.

"I'm so sorry, Silas, but I didn't know who else to call." The static on his phone line, which he has never called the phone company out to fix, makes every sentence an effort. Cheryl tries to keep it simple, but just explaining everything to him out loud makes her choke up.

Silas is horrified at her predicament, and his anger is not just at Bointy. "You let them give you a lie detector test? They're as bad as the damn SS. Everything's rigged. Don't you know anything?"

Suddenly, Cheryl's a little girl again—ashamed, stupid, worthless. "I'm sorry. Just forget it." She's ready to hang up.

Silas nearly yells back into the phone. "What are you talking about? Tell that Chief to pick me up right now so I can come down there and get you." Then a firm warning. "And don't say another word to them."

After she hangs up, she looks sheepishly at Chief Bointy.

"He says you need to pick him up so he can come get me?"

"Oh, good grief," Bointy laughs.

Shelby scoffs. "Go get *him*? That's ridiculous."

"If I don't, he'll get his damn boat out of storage and get behind the wheel." The "boat" is Silas's '75 Buick, no longer pristine after Silas backed its enormous rear end into three different cars last year. Bointy unofficially banned him from driving in Medicine Wheel, Silas's current Driver's License notwithstanding.

"I'll swing by and get him when I've finished talking to Buddy Mason." Bointy heads out the door.

While Bointy is out consulting with the District Attorney Mason, Assistant Chief Myers minds the fort up front, around the corner from her cell, so she can't see him. Since the moment he locked Cheryl inside, perspiration has been rolling down her back, in spite of the cool autumn morning.

Remembering Silas's words makes her even more miserable. *You did this to yourself, you idiot.* She paces, stopping occasionally to white-knuckle the cell bars. She can hear Shelby talking on the office phone in a low voice, and, later, crinkling sounds, like from a potato chip bag. Other than that, and her own pounding heart, it is quiet as a cave.

It's been half an hour since she talked to Silas, but nothing yet. Shelby saunters back into the cell area, baloney sandwich in one hand and a smoking cigarette in the other.

"You want anything to eat?" Before she can answer, he looks at her with concern. "Are you okay? You look pale . . . ."

"Whew . . . I never thought of myself as claustrophobic, but this is unnerving."

He takes a casual drag from his cigarette. "Yeah. But I guess that's the idea of being behind bars, huh?"

It occurs to her that Silas was right. This guy would be perfect as a smarmy SS officer in a WWII movie.

Apparently reading her annoyance, Myers moves closer to the bars. "Hey, I didn't mean anything but that. Sometimes I can be . . .." Lost, he looks around as though the air might tell him what to say next. "Could I . . . I mean, would it help if I sat back here with you?"

"That'd be okay, yeah," Cheryl finally says. Even someone she doesn't exactly like might help this feeling of helplessness. When she was arrested three years ago, too badly injured to move, she woke up in a hospital, so she had missed the chilling experience of lockdown back then.

He pulls a wooden chair in from the office area and sits down on the wall opposite the cell. He stubs his cigarette out on the cement floor, then puts the butt in his pocket. "Not supposed to smoke in here," he says.

"It's nice that you pick up your butts," she says, as a sort of peace gesture. They really have nothing to say to one another, but she manages a smile.

"I guess you know, you sure could help us out if you have any ideas on what Miss Lawrence was hiding."

"Hiding?"

"The way the place was tossed . . . indicates somebody

was after something."

"She never told me about anything like that. Of course, Effie was a very private person. She was of that generation."

"Still, you lived next door to her. Surely, she must have said something, even if you didn't realize what it meant at the time."

"I never thought of her as a lady of mystery."

"Maybe she had millions socks away that nobody knows about."

The phone rings and Shelby jumps to get it. When he returns after a minute, he announces, "Chief's on his way back. He's got Mr. Weintraub with him."

Only a few minutes later, Cheryl hears Silas's booming voice. He hurries back to the cell and looks anxiously at her. "You alright, Cheryl?"

She grips the cell bars. "I'm fine, just get me out of here."

"Don't worry, I'm going to take care of it," he assures her. "But prepare yourself. It's not good news."

"What does that mean?"

"I thought they'd release you to me, but that short-pants D.A. has other ideas."

At this point, Chief Bointy, ducking his head, makes his way back to the cell. "Well, like I told Silas, I didn't see things going this way, but it's Buddy Mason's call.

"Will someone tell me what's happening?" Cheryl asks.

Bointy avoids her eyes. "Cheryl Jackson, you're under arrest for conspiracy to commit murder."

Cheryl is speechless.

Silas is not. "How does that dumb little squirt figure conspiracy?"

Bointy does not appear anxious to defend the D.A., but he isn't about to get into a verbal scuffle with Silas, either. "All I know is—and I'm not going to discuss this with you now, Silas—he sees prior convictions here, motive and opportunity. He's out there right now announcing it in time for the news at noon."

"It's the Gestapo, *déjà vu* all over again," Silas declares loudly.

"Except she's got a hearing in District Court at 4:30 today for bail," Bointy announces. "With any luck, Cheryl, you might be home in time for dinner."

Cheryl stands frozen until Silas takes her hand. He turns to Bointy.

"Can I speak to her in private a minute, Asa?"

Bointy nods and he and Shelby shuffle outside for another smoke.

Silas lowers his voice. "Now listen, my niece in Oklahoma City called me. The lawyer. She saw it on the news."

The one who got out of law school recently?"

"Yeah, I told her we need a good one." Silas pats her

cheek. "She's going to find us the best."

Four hours later, the Chief lets Cheryl ride without handcuffs to the District Court in Lawton. She feels doubly grateful to him when she sees several Medicine Wheel gawkers, casually hanging near the entrance to catch sight of the accused walking inside. The news had spread faster than a bad virus.

Cheryl shudders when she spots Doyle Lowe just inside the front doors. Of all people, of course, her ex shows up. Always glad to give himself an early afternoon off from his auto window-tint business.

It is actually a relief to get inside the courtroom, with its ancient oak woodwork and dusty photographs of dead judges lining the walls. Bointy leads her to the back where, he explains, they will stay until called.

Silas is already seated in the gallery, checking the court entrance every few seconds. He gives her a grin and a thumbs up. His niece must have found an attorney to represent her.

The ambitious prosecutor, Buddy Mason, is already in place and currently handling the charges on a dock of defendants, from domestic abuse to aggravated assault and battery. Buddy is variously described as a "pistol" or "go-getter" by older men in the area. Women, however, tend to see a pushy guy with a "short-man syndrome." But everyone would agree his snappy beige suit and green silk tie suggest he has bigger plans than remaining prosecutor in Comanche County.

When "State of Oklahoma vs. Cheryl Jackson" is called, Bointy brings her up to the area in front of the dais. It is just the two of them. Cheryl looks around for Silas, but he's headed toward the entrance doors, apparently to search outside.

Judge Paul Chibitty, a Comanche icon with a sagging, pockmarked face, nods sternly at Cheryl. Then he looks to Chief Bointy with upraised eyebrows. "Is Counsel present?"

Bointy shrugs. "They were supposed to meet us here, Your Honor." "Miss Jackson, do you have counsel?" Chibitty's voice is crushed sand.

"I believe so, Your Honor." She glances back toward Silas, but he has gone outside.

The Judge makes a point of checking his wristwatch, then purses his lips. "I'm supposed to be at a baptism in thirty minutes, folks."

As if on cue, the doors swing open at the back and a woman in a black suit and tortoise shell glasses sweeps in, red hair flying behind her. Silas is on her heels. She looks around at everyone in the court, who by this time are all staring back at her.

"The Jackson hearing?"

Judge Chibitty nods. "And you are?"

Josey Spangler, Your Honor, for the defense."

"You're late," the judge scolds.

"I'm sorry, Your Honor, I beg the court's forgiveness. I hurried here from Oklahoma City this afternoon as fast as I could. You work fast in this part of the state."

She nods at Silas, who returns to his seat, while she walks, smiling, to Cheryl's side.

"All the way from the city," Chibitty observes dryly to no

one in particular.

"Silas Weintraub's niece, yes, from Oklahoma City. Under the circumstances, may I have ten minutes with my client, Your Honor?"

"Make it five. I've got to get to church." He pounds the gavel and retires to his chambers for the interim.

Josey and Cheryl sit down at the defense counsel table. Silas takes this as his cue to join them. He squints through his thick glasses at Karen.

"I wouldn't have known you with all that long hair," he says, shaking his head. "How many years has it been?"

"At least ten," Josey says. "I've been trying to get down here to see you since I moved back to the city last year."

"How old are you now? Thirty?"

"You know I didn't even start law school until I was almost forty, but thank you." Josey pats his hand fondly. "And you, well, you don't look a day older."

Silas grins. "That law school taught you how to lie, I see."

She chuckles, then turns serious. "I've only got a couple of minutes with Cheryl, Uncle Silas." He takes the hint and scoots back to his seat.

Josey offers her hand to shake. "Cheryl, nice to meet you." Her flashing eyes and the snappy way she gets into her briefcase are all business. "My uncle gave me the general circumstances over the phone."

"I appreciate you coming."

"Sorry to have to meet you this way, Ms. Jackson. Now here is what's going to happen. You will plead Not Guilty when the court asks, and then I will argue for your release. Don't say anything else or speak to anyone until we can have a sit down, okay?"

Cheryl nods agreement, relieved to have a lawyer do the heavy lifting. Before she can blink, the Judge enters the courtroom and takes his place.

Reading of the charges is waived and, when prompted, Cheryl stands and says, "Not Guilty, Your Honor."

The judge nods. "I will hear brief—and I do mean brief—arguments on bail."

Buddy Mason spreads his arms. "Due to the heinous nature of this crime--"

Chibitty is already ahead of him. "Etc., etc. How much, Counsel?"

Deflated, but recognizing an impatient judge, he says, "State asks fifty thousand dollars."

Josey springs out of her seat, appropriately indignant. "Defendant has lived here almost all her life, Your Honor, and doesn't have the means to flee. All she wants is to clear her name. Her own recognizance should . . . ."

"Split the difference," Chibitty says with a bounce of his gavel. "Twenty-five thousand cash bond. Dismissed." His robe is practically off before he disappears from the courtroom.

Prosecutor Buddy Mason stands open mouthed then

closes it with a shrug.

Josey looks stunned at the speed of her success, while Cheryl is wondering how the fact that she's on parole was never brought up. Had Bointy not mentioned it to the D.A.? If so, Cheryl is grateful, but it doesn't make her any closer to getting out. She tells her new lawyer, "Hate to say it, but it might as well be a million."

Josey grins. "No problem. Uncle Silas has it covered. We'll have you out in an hour."

"Get real. Silas doesn't have that kind of money."

"You're kidding, right? My uncle dealt in amber when he lived in Poland, and he's still got a finger in the turquoise business around here. Don't let the tattered sweater fool you."

An hour later Cheryl Jackson is out.

CHAPTER THIRTEEN

When Silas, Josey and Cheryl get back to the R.V. Village, Cheryl notices the Boney sisters peeking between their blinds to get a glimpse of the accused murderer—the same person, they must be horrified to realize, that they trusted with their bank deposits only yesterday. And suddenly, a couple of other retirees need to check their mail, casting curious eyes at Cheryl as they pass by. The grapevine is alive and humming.

Once they get inside Silas's place, Cheryl realizes it's the first place she's felt safe since morning. Exhaustion sinks her like a stone. She can barely keep her eyes open, not that it stops her from wanting a drink in the worst way.

Josey insists they all talk right away. Silas puts the yapping Chihuahua pack out in their pens so they can hear one another inside. Then he jumps into preparing breakfast for supper, which is what the evening meal is called by most locals. He rebuffs the women's protests.

"I want to cook for two of my favorite ladies. You two talk."

By the time Cheryl updates Josey with the details of her statement to Chief Bointy, aided by Silas's interruptions when she leaves anything out, supper is served. It's the next best thing to a drink. Silas's specialty is scrambling eggs just right and frying up bacon and crispy hash browns, the old-fashioned kind of breakfast people chowed down on before cholesterol counts.

Later, nerve endings relaxed, and a warm stomach pooched out, Cheryl has to force herself to get up and start washing the dishes.

Silas, bits of egg on his shirt front, studies his niece with a grin. "You sound so much more mature, Josie. They must've taught you to talk like a lawyer."

"They made all us gals lower our voices. God forbid we should sound shrill in court."

They all laugh. It's sweet to see them together. Cheryl had not met Silas's sister and her American husband before they died in a car accident a number of years back, and barely remembered they had a daughter. They brought Silas along with them to the states when they moved to Tulsa, but he was still a village boy at heart and eventually ended up in Medicine Wheel through his interest in Native jewelry.

When they finish reminiscing, Cheryl tells Silas, "I'll never be able to thank you for getting me out today. I will pay you back somehow."

"Oh, shut up. What am I going to do with money? Spend it on these damn dogs? Besides, my niece needs the work, new law practice and all." He grins at Josey, who colors a little.

"It's true. When I saw it on the noon news, I remembered Uncle Silas talking about Miss Lawrence, so I called and he said you need a lawyer and . . . well, synchronicity, huh? I'm still building my practice in the city, and I couldn't think of anybody who could get down here today to help you out."

"Are you in criminal law?" Cheryl asks.

"No, but I can represent you until we find somebody who is."

"Whoever found out her secret killed her" Silas announces. "I told the Chief that right off."

"Effie? Secrets?" Cheryl raises her eyebrows.

"I couldn't talk about them until now. I promised her."

Silas goes on alert, locking the front door and peeking out the windows. He opens an overhead compartment in the dining nook and retrieves a screwdriver from his tool kit.

"Can I help, Silas?" Cheryl offers.

"Nope. I got it." In a few moments, he has unscrewed a small panel that houses a hidden slot. Carefully, he pulls out an object wrapped in a pillowcase.

"It's time you saw this, anyway," he says and lifts a carved cedar box. "Effie gave this to me last summer." He takes a chain from around his neck, which has a key on it and hands it to Cheryl.

"Open it. Effie knew if her good-for-nothin' relatives found out about this, they'd try to get their hands on it for sure. She hid it in her safety deposit box at the bank for years until Cliff started sniffing around.

Cheryl unlocks the box. She can almost smell the age of the contents. A yellowed envelope lies inside. Underneath that a leather map just fits in the box. For a moment, even the room seems to hold its breath.

"Read the letter first, Cheryl," Silas says. "Then we'll get to the map."

She is almost afraid to touch it. The paper looks as though it might crumble. Gingerly, she unfolds the onion-skin pages. The cursive writing from an ink pen is small and precise—a woman's hand.

"3-18-1940. To Whom It May Concern: These are the true events of October 1, 1939, when I was a nurse on the night shift at Lawton Hospital."

"Wow, fifty years ago," Cheryl says in amazement.

"I was called to the bedside of Charlie Edgars, an old

prospector who was admitted following a bad fall in the mountains. The doctors deemed his situation hopeless due to internal hemorrhaging. We were just trying to keep him comfortable until the inevitable.

"In the middle of the night he became quite agitated, coughing up blood and barely able to breathe. He knew he was dying and begged me to bring him his pack. I retrieved a rolled-up leather map from one of the compartments. Its markings had been burned in with red hot wire, he told me.

"About forty years earlier, while prospecting in the Mt. Scott area, Mr. Edgars told me he had seen, through his looking glass, a stranger in a cattle coat digging a hole, from which he retrieved a metal box. The stranger carefully made sure he wasn't being watched before opening it, Edgars said."

"Wow, right around here," Josey says.

Silas nods then says, "Keep reading, Cheryl."

"Charlie Edgars sneaked up nearer to the spot and watch the stranger bury the box again, fill in the hole and roll a large rock with double humps on top of the spot. But from his closer distance, seeing him through his looking glass, the prospector knew the stranger instantly, had no doubt who it was. In spite of his new suit and hat, Edgars recognized Frank James, Jesse's brother, fresh out of jail."

Cheryl stops. You mean, Frank James—the Frank James—was burying treasure?"

Silas sighs at her. "No, honey, don't act dumb. He was digging it up. Outlaws had loot buried everywhere in these mountains. Safest place for it."

Josey smiles. "I guess they couldn't very well put it in a bank."

"Right. And they couldn't get caught carrying it neither.

In Frank's case, it was his retirement plan. He would dig up his blood money—as needed."

"Edgars hid some distance away and waited until James was long gone," Cheryl continues, *"then shoveled out the fresh dirt under the rock. He found a metal strongbox filled with Mexican coins, each one worth fifty dollars, he told me."*

"That's how they laundered their money in the old days. Traded it in to Mexico coin dealers."

"Charlie Edgars was too scared to take but a few coins, knowing the James boys. But he did burn a map of the location into a piece of rawhide."

Silas, with some ceremony, carefully unrolls the ancient leather map. It is difficult to decipher what the difference icons might mean. The double humped rock seems to be a crude "M" shape marked "BR."

Did you find the treasure, Uncle Silas?"

Silas shakes his head. "Effie Lawrence was a strict Christian lady. She didn't give me this so I could go treasure hunting. You'd better finish that letter."

Cheryl reads on. *"Even after Frank James died, Edgars only took a handful of coins at a time, cashing them in places where he wasn't known, for fear of being discovered by one of the many James descendants, who were always on the lookout for more booty. Edgars himself planned to pass the map on to his only nephew but died in a sudden seizure before he could give me the name."*

Both Silas and Josey are pinned on her every word. *"I have been sore at heart . . . ."* Cheryl pauses as she notices Silas mouthing this part with her as she reads. He awkwardly swipes away a tear.

"I have wept and prayed over the weight of this

knowledge, for this is blood money, taken from wounded or dying victims by evil men. It is a sin to accept it or give it away. The Lord has told me it should stay buried, even as the sins that earned it. I must safeguard its hiding place forever, lest others use it for their own selfish gain."

Both women stare in disbelief at Silas. Josey asks, "Are you telling us that no one ever even checked this map out?"

"She'd have none of it," Silas says, holding his head high. "I honored her wishes."

"But, Silas," Cheryl asks, "why didn't she just turn it over to the Police?"

"Effie swore everybody in this area back then was a treasure hunter—including the police. Still could be, far as I know. Like they say, 'you can't trust anybody when it comes to gold.'"

"If she was so religious, why not find it and give it to the church?" Josey asks.

"The blood money thing, I bet," Cheryl says. "People used to think money like that was cursed. If you used it, awful things would happen."

Silas nods. "She also thought her minister's eyes lit up a little too much when she hinted at a lot of money. So she prayed for a sign, she said, a message that would tell her what to do."

"And . . .?" Josey leans forward.

"At some point, Effie had a powerful dream, she told me, and the Lord appeared to her and said to wait, that when the time was right, she would know exactly what to do with the map. But, until then, keep it safe."

"It all sounds so . . . well, biblical," Cheryl says, trying to subdue her own secret excitement at the prospect of treasure.

"Effie never got that sign, and she believed that was God's way of telling her that the map to this blood money should never see the light of day."

"So, why are you showing us now?" Cheryl asks.

It looks as though Silas might burst from his misery. "Because damn it, she let them cut her toes off before she'd tell I was the one who had it. She would have told them everything, otherwise. She died to keep them away from me."

"Silas, you can't blame yourself." Cheryl puts her hand on his arm.

"I can and do. No way she would've let them do that to her if she'd still had the map. She'd have given it up."

"She loved you, Uncle Silas. You'd have done the same for her."

"I don't know if that's true or not." Silas pulls himself together and looks from one to the other. "Now I'm too old and crippled up to go after them. And these stumblebums we've got for police won't do anything, especially now that they're sure you did it, Cheryl. It's up to you two."

"The two of us?" Josey asks, looking sideways at Cheryl.

"That's right. Anybody else here?"

Cheryl is astonished. "We're not investigators, Silas. We couldn't--"

"You're both smart . . . most of the time, anyway. How else do you think you're gonna stay out of jail, Cheryl? Hope for them goof-ups to stumble onto the truth?"

The women chuckle at his bluntness, but Cheryl wonders if he isn't depressingly close to the truth. "He's right about that. The investigation's probably closed now, at least as far as Buddy

Mason is concerned.

Silas looks at her with his jaw jutted forward. "You figure out who started nosing around, looking for that old map last year, and that'll be Effie's killer.

CHAPTER FOURTEEN

Rumbling gray clouds drifted low in the sky the next morning. The forecast for rain doesn't deter Cheryl's plan for the day. In the R.V. Village residents will use the inconvenience as a chance to sit on the front porch and watch it come down. But Cheryl is already out, driving through it.

Her pickup kicks up moist red dust as it tools down a country road. Her lawyer rides shotgun, puzzling over scribbled instructions as she watches for the only landmark supposedly visible from the road, a rusting cattle gate.

"We haven't seen a single one," Josey complains. A mile later, she says, "Who is this guy anyway?"

Cheryl's no help. "Silas says he's the best guide in the area. He's the best hidden one, that's for sure."

The pickup rolls by a stretch of barbed wire fence, a crude, hand painted sign pops up on a fencepost: *"NO TRESPASSERS ALLOWED."*

An old cattle gate appears, nearly shrouded in vines and almost hidden in the shade. Cheryl slams the brakes and slowly pulls over to the dirt shoulder. "There it is."

"Good eye," Josey says. "I would've missed that completely."

"I nearly did."

Josey jumps out of the truck ahead of Cheryl and starts pulling the rain-soaked foliage away to find the gate latch. "Where does it open?" She lifts up more of the burgundy and yellow vines to see better.

Coming up behind her, Cheryl realizes, too late, what Josey has hold of. She gasps, "Wait, that's--"

From some trees behind the fence, horse's hooves approach the gate, startling them. A male voice warns, "Careful. That's poison."

They both jump, and Josey instinctively puts her hand to her mouth.

"Don't touch your face," Cheryl says . . . again too late.

A lanky Native American, mid-thirties, in jeans and waterproof windbreaker, with leather strap-wrapped braids, pulls up his pinto on the other side of the gate. His stoic face barely betrays a touch of amusement. For a second, Cheryl thinks he looks familiar. Maybe someone she has seen in town at some point.

Josey looks in panic at her hands, then turns belligerent. "What the hell are you doing putting poison on a public gate?"

"It grows there. Poison oak. Afraid I haven't kept it cut back very well." He dismounts and walks toward them.

Josey is not pacified. "Well, that's just grand."

"Sorry. Do you have a first aid kit in your truck?" he asks.

"Not one that would help this," Cheryl says. "Maybe

there's some Neosporin."

"Come on up to the house. I'll concoct something." He seems friendly enough, and poison oak always needs treatment sooner rather than later.

"Very generous," Cheryl says for the two of them. He opens the gate with some leather gloves from the waistband of his jeans.

The rain stops as he leads their truck up the dirt driveway to an aging white frame house. It stands on a hill beside ricks of wood. Besides an old working Nissan, there are a couple of cars from the 60's, propped up on cement blocks, waiting to be restored, it looks like.

Cheryl smiles and shakes her head. I*s there a farm in a hundred miles that doesn't have a little cemetery of rusted old cars up on blocks?*

As soon as they park, he dismounts, and some hunting dogs appear, smelling around the pickup tires. One hikes his leg.

"Don't be rude, Bear," the man tells his dog, too late. "Sorry," he says over his shoulder, "he's got a mind of his own." He turns to them. "I'm Noah Frejo, by the way."

Cheryl and Josey introduce themselves as they move into a simple, uncluttered living room. Hives are already beginning to erupt on Josey's fine-skinned, ivory cheeks. She sees a mirror and studies with horror the tiny bubbles on her face. "This is bad, you guys. Really bad."

"Wow," Cheryl says, trying not to look too horrified. "I've never seen such a fast reaction. You must be allergic."

"I don't know," Josey says, panic in her voice.

"Looks like it. I'll find something." Noah disappears down the hall.

Cheryl gives a sympathetic smile to Josey as they wait. On one wall is a display of Natives, circa 1890's, as well as arrangements of natural objects, bones, feathers—like dreamcatchers, but more serious looking.

Josey wrinkles her nose. "Is that dog pee I smell?"

"I don't notice anything."

A contemporary wedding photo of Noah and a Native woman, both in traditional dress, sits on a bureau. And beside it, a small canvas bag with painted objects. It looks like a medicine bundle, which holds power symbols or objects that stand for strength to the owner.

Josey paces nervously. "I'm itching like crazy. What's he got? I hope it's not some nasty Indian salve."

"Be grateful for anything. You're puffing up like a blowfish. And whatever it is, even it's a stinky poultice, just put it on and don't say a word."

Noah enters, squinting at the label on a small bottle. "Here, this might help."

"What is it?" Josey suspiciously narrows her puffy eyes.

"Calamine lotion. Sorry, I'm all out of the prescription stuff."

Cheryl smiles to herself. *I like this guy already.*

A half-hour later, they sit in a row of plastic bucket seats in the Emergency Room of Southwestern Medical Center in Lawton, while a doctor checks Josey out. It doesn't take long.

A Native American, Dr. Hokeah, comes into the area and eyes them. "You're with Miss Spangler?" They nod. "She's had a severe allergic reaction to the poison oak. I've got a poultice on her, but I'd like to monitor her until evening at least, in case of swelling in her airways."

Cheryl feels relieved to be free of responsibility. "No problem," she assures him. After he leaves, she turns to Noah. "You probably need to get home to your family."

He looks surprised. "I live alone."

"Oh, I saw the wedding picture. I just assumed . . . .."

"My wife's . . . gone."

"Oh, well, in that case . . . can I buy you a cup of coffee? Explain my problem?"

On the way back to Medicine Wheel, the rain starts again, splattering the windshield. By the time they get there, the gutters of the old brick streets are running with water.

A fading sign in front of the Big Chief Diner still displays the remnants of a painted war chief whooping it up. Inside, the place hums with a mixture of locals, Natives, and rednecks, many of whom look up when Cheryl and Noah walk in.

Not shy about staring at the person accused of helping murder Effie, Cheryl notices. *Lord-a-mighty, get an eyeful, why don't you?*

Noah signals a waitress for two coffees. "I know I haven't turned into a celebrity overnight," he says. "Is it you?"

Turning red, Cheryl explains about the obstruction and conspiracy charge and getting bailed out. "Silas recommended you to get us on the right track. He says it's up to me to find out what happened. And that Chief Bointyy won't because he's in over his head."

The waitress openly flirts with Noah as she plops down their coffees. "Anything else, y'all?"

Noah smiles at her. "Not right now, thanks." When she leaves, he turns back to Cheryl. "I was sorry to hear about Miss Lawrence. It sounded like a vicious killing."

She has to swallow back a burst of emotion at Effie's name.

Noah breaks the silence. "How is old Silas? Haven't run into him in a while."

"Feisty as ever. How do you know him?"

"About ten years ago, I introduced him around to some turquoise dealers. He handled amber when he was in Poland, he said, but the native stones caught his interest here, apparently. We've sort of stayed in touch."

Cheryl looks around at people at the tables, some still whispering and stealing glances at her. Suddenly she's embarrassed by the entire place, with its thoughtless redskin mentality.

"Jees, this place. Sorry. I should have thought of how you'd feel about it."

He grins. "It is pretty politically incorrect."

"Pathetically incorrect. I'm sorry. Why don't we go somewhere else?"

"I'd love to, but their coffee costs more and isn't as good." Noah chuckles and shrugs. "You have to pick your battles, huh?"

"I guess so. Do you go to Crazy Horse Saloon?"

"No, that's easy, though. I don't drink. But gassing up jmy car, well, that's a tough one."

"Oh wow." She laughs and cringes at the same time. "The Heap Big Wampum on the other side of the highway."

He laughs good-naturedly. "And that one's owned by one of us."

Cheryl notices how everything in his long face seems to work: soft brown eyes, sprinkles of acne scars, a Roman nose.

"I decided a long time ago that you can't get mad about everything," he says. "My friends who did are either in prison or dead."

The waitress brings their coffees, and he nods a thanks.

"So, you went to a lot of trouble to hunt me up. What've I got to do with what you're working on?"

She is ready to get back on point. "Silas says you're the best guide in these parts. Especially on treasure hunters and lose claims."

He nods. "Okay, who or what are you looking for?"

"Rare coins. From a long time ago. I need to find out who's been trying to get their hands on the map to a specific treasure. A prospector named Charlie Edgars first found it." She figures that will will his appetite.

He sips his coffee and nods. "Ah, Edgars. You must mean the Frank James booty."

Cheryl is taken aback. "You mean you've already heard of it?"

"Sure, it's well known in treasure circles. But there hasn't been any movement on that map in . . . I can't remember the last time I heard anybody mention it. But that doesn't necessarily mean anything."

She leans forward and speaks low. "It turns out Effie Lawrence has been hiding the original map for years."

That perks him up. "They think someone killed her because of the map?"

"Effie was Charlie Edgars' nurse the night he died. He gave it to her on his deathbed."

He stares at her. "I never heard that. I mean, it was rumored someone on the hospital staff might've taken it, but the authorities kept their names top secret, for their own safety. So, you need someone to authenticate the map for you? I'd love to."

Cheryl is not ready to be completely open with him yet. Josey had said they should put the map back in her uncle's hiding place, for fear of something happening to it. "My lawyer wouldn't let me bring it today."

Noah shrugs. "Then . . . I don't understand what I can do

for you."

"They tortured Effie to try and find it. I need help to find out who is looking for it. Someone desperate or greedy enough to kill for it."

"Hundreds of people have nosed around about the Edgars and James treasure. It's in all the outlaw treasure stories."

"This would be recently, in the last year or so. They might have been pushy, persistent."

Noah gives a knowing chuckle. "Cheryl, I've met treasure hunters who'd eat their own young for an authentic map. For all I know, you could be one of them."

If his tone weren't so light, she might feel insulted. She looks out the window for a moment at the steady rain, then says simply, "I'd never do that."

He's still grinning. "Neither would I. But I can't risk my contacts on someone who's just bluffing, either."

"I see your point." Cheryl considers a moment. "Okay, I'll have to trust Silas's judgment. He did vouch for you." She glances around the room and sees the customers seem to have turned back to their own business. Surreptitiously pulling the wrapped leather map out of her purse, she lays it on the table. "My lawyer would kill me if she knew I brought this."

Noah lightly unrolls it and touches the ancient rawhide with reverence. "This looks like a real museum piece. I'm sorry I don't have latex gloves with me." He studies it carefully for a few minutes.

He points to a spot on the map. "This is the Wildlife

Refuge area now."

"How do you know?"

"The big spiral? That's Mount Scott, standard symbol, pretty much."

"Well, that's good, isn't it?"

"Sure, it just doesn't set it apart from the others all that much."

"Others?" *What on earth is he talking about?*

"Frank James was associated with a number of buried treasures."

"Oh?" Suddenly, she feels stupid and unprepared.

"There was plenty of it buried in the Wichita's, supposedly. One time Frank dug up six thousand dollars near Cache, and that's 1800's money we're talking about. And that's just one of a half a dozen stories.

Cheryl is fascinated. She points at the map. "The letter Effie wrote about the old prospector seeing James at this site said he was in a new suit and just out of prison."

"That could help us." Noah nods his head back and forth as he thinks on it. "That old scoundrel. Everybody knew Frank James had to have more going for him after prison than selling shoes and doing gigs in wild west shows. Besides, nothing so romantic as living off buried loot. Do you have a date for this map?"

"Effie got it in 1939, and it was maybe forty years old

then. That would make it, sheesh, about ninety years old?"

"Amazing. These groupings here show Elk Mountain and Charon Gardens, and there's a clear legend for direction. These trees and other markings, after this long, they're gone now. It's not all that much to go on, really."

It takes a moment for Cheryl to digest what Noah says. Outside the rain lets up, leaving a sheen on the streets. "But, if that is the case, why would anybody kill for it?"

I don't know. Maybe they don't know much about historical maps. There's plenty of greenhorns out there."

"But how about this landmark? 'B.R.' Surely that's a big clue. Isn't it?"

Noah smiles and shakes her head with what she senses is pity. She does not appreciate being patronized, especially when she was just finding him interesting. "What?"

"No offense, but you really are a beginner. Come on. I'll show you Butt Rock. On the house."

CHAPTER FIFTEEN

Noah never tires of riding through the curving roads of the Wichita Wildlife Refuge, only a few miles from Medicine Wheel. Today the cleansing shower has deepened the rich greens and browns of the trees and grasses and left a wet gloss on the mountain boulders.

As Cheryl chauffeurs them down the narrow two-lane, pink-tipped grass blades on the shoulders dance away from the pickup tires. An earth tremor barely registers with either of them, though the seismograph at nearby Meers, home of the Buffalo Burger, does an uptick. They tend to be numerous in the area, but at such low readings, almost nobody takes note.

They ride in silence as buffalo, longhorns, deer and elk look up to stare, probably wondering why humans and their belching machines keep barging into their home. Past Mount Scott, with its paved road coiling around it like a rattlesnake, Noah points to a sign. "Turn left up here."

"We going to Charon Gardens?" Cheryl asks.

"Yeah. You know it?"

"Sure, I come around here quite a bit."

A few miles down the road, red stone rocks form a circle around a manmade parking lot for visitors.

"Park anywhere," Noah says and gets out of the pickup,

pointing to a spot ahead of them. "Come on."

Cheryl looks impatient with this waste of time but gets out and follows him. "You know, I do have other things I need to be doing. I can't just be running around."

As Noah walks ahead of her on a path to the side of the parking area, he can't help but think that she hasn't changed all that much. Still stubborn and smart mouthed. Still athletic, despite a limp on one of those long pony legs that he had loved to watch running around the basketball court.

"You better not be putting me on." She chuckles, but her voice has a little edge.

"Almost there." Ten feet farther, he stops on a flat butte where people can sit on a cluster of rocks and look over the blue water below. He pushes aside some overgrown bushes and nods to her. "Right there."

Partially obscured by foliage, a rock nearly four feet wide and as high as Cheryl's waist, boasts two large humps on top. It looks uncannily like the rear view of someone bending over to touch their toes. It is nearly covered with teenage carvings: "T luvs E, L.S. & A.G., Nell puts out."

Her face turns lobster red. "I can't believe I never saw this before."

Noah shrugs, no big deal. "There's probably a dozen butt rocks around, but this is the famous one. Nobody knows just where it was moved from. In the 60's sometime. A midnight requisition. You never hung out here in high school?"

"With my mother? Not on your life."

"That's right. A good girl, straight A's?"

She nods, studying the rock. "I feel pretty stupid now."

"No reason to. A map that old? They're impossible. The way the land shifts. What used to be by a river isn't anymore. There're years of erosion. Old maps are are rarely that helpful."

"So it's . . . Effie must not have known any of this." She looks as if she might cry. "Did she die for something worthless?"

Now Noah feels awful. "No, listen—look, it's the real thing. It's just not that useful at this point. Even if we tracked down every 'Butt Rock' in the region, who knows if it would give us anything. But now that I know it's the real deal, let's go talk to somebody who might know if anybody's been snooping around about it lately."

A half hour later they are back in town at Cracker's Country Store, one of the few truly ancient "junk" stores left in Medicine Wheel. Behind a dingy picture window, everything from plastic flowers to books to tourist trinkets are displayed, most of which looks like it hasn't been repositioned or dusted for years. An antique oak showcase runs almost the length of the store and displays the valuable wares, from priceless antique knives to carved wooden art.

Jake "Cracker" Box, the owner, an enormous man with a ruddy drinker's nose and small dark eyes, almost disappeared in his puffy face, rules from his throne, a stool perched behind his cash register, circa 1950's. A lot of locals shun going inside now, because Cracker is still a defiant smoker and, as owner, he does what he wants, and hell take the hind quarter.

It doesn't really annoy Noah. He figures when you think

of the things people do to each other in this world, smoking doesn't rank that high in his book. Still, the store does always have an oily, smoky smell clinging everywhere.

Cracker gives a wave. "Well, haven't seen you in a coon's age, Noah."

"I get to town every now and again," Noah says. They make small talk, mainly weather and sports, while Noah explains they are looking into the Edgars story, which sets Cracker on a roll.

Cheryl is cracking the spine of Oklahoma Hidden Treasures, by Jake "Cracker" Box, Jr. Himself, when he comes up behind her.

"Treasure, huh?" he says, causing her to jump. "Yessir, you'd be surprised how many people've got a hidden loot story from these parts. But the name Charlie Edgars . . . that's something else again." He sees her blow dust from his book and grins. "You've got a good eye, young lady."

"You know Cheryl Jackson, don't you, Cracker?" Noah asks.

"Who doesn't know the All-Star basketball player? State champions—when was that? Fifteen years ago?"

"Seventeen, actually. '72."

"Right. Shot the winning basket with 3 seconds to go." He studies her. "I remember your folks, too. Where are they now?"

"They sold their house and bought a big rig R.V. They travel all around the country now." She points to his book. "Is

Charlie Edgars in here?"

"Yes, ma'am the whole story. Page 312. Wait, no, 315, it is. Back in the day, Edgars himself hung around here all the time."

Cheryl looks dubious. "We're talking the 30's, now."

Cracker is undeterred. "He was a friend of my dad's. Didn't Noah tell you? In fact, when I was a kid, I found Edgars and my old man down in the basement one time, drunk as skunks. My dad was goin' after him. How he's full of crap and don't know a valuable coin from a hole in the ground. So, Edgars puffs all up and starts to struttin' around and, quick as a drunk man can, that old bugger pulled a gold coin out of his pocket that . . . well, it sure as hell shut my daddy. Honest Injun."

She glances at Noah, who takes the remark in stride, then back to Cracker. "Where did he say it came from?"

"If I knew that, I wouldn't be selling plastic flowers, now would I?" When Cracker stops laughing at his own joke, he adds on a more somber note. "A few years later, Edgars was dead."

From somewhere below them, they hear muffled thumps. Cracker shakes his head good-naturedly and walks over to the top of a large stairway going down. "You damn dogs," he hollers to below, "settle down, down there." He shoots them a sidelong grin. "They get frisky when the bitch is in heat."

Noah studies Cracker's wily, wrinkled visage, with its hound dog jowls flopping down over both jaws. "So nobody's sniffed around about the James booty, huh?"

"Can't say there has been. Wish I could help."

Cheryl walks up to the counter with Cracker's book. "This says the doctor who treated Charlie Edgars was attacked?"

Cracker nods. "Yep, beat up bad. Nearly died. It's all in the book."

"Guess I'd better buy one then." Cheryl fishes money out of her purse. Pleased, Cracker takes the book and blows off the dust accumulated on the cover. The ancient cash register gives an old-fashioned ring when he opens and closes it.

As Noah and Cheryl drive away, Cracker waves through the window, then turns the sign on the door from Open to Closed.

"He's closing up?" Cheryl asks. "It's barely afternoon."

Probably got a fishing date. Cracker's store, Cracker's hours."

Cheryl checks her watch. "I'd better call the hospital, check on Josey."

"They've got a phone up in the hotel."

"Good idea."

CHAPTER SIXTEEN

Cheryl figures if Noah's with her, it will keep her from drifting into the hotel bar just across from the restaurant. Even she has that much pride left. If she can keep it up, this will be Day 2 without booze. But not without the chronic pain that creeps into her leg when it's damp and cool like today. Even the walk at Charon Gardens started her bad leg aching. Now it feels like it's on fire.

As Noah gets a booth and orders them both cheeseburgers, Cheryl calls Southwest Memorial on the hotel phone. They tell her they will release Josey if somebody can stay with her.

"We can pick up Josey at the hospital any time," she tells Noah when she joins him. "Her vision is still impaired from the swelling. I told them I'd drive her to Silas's place. I called him to see if that's okay, but he's not answering. Must have got a wild hair." Cheryl realizes she's jabbering, like she does when the leg pain is over the top.

Noah nods and goes back to Cracker's book.

"Finding anything?" she asks.

"Just reading about Edgars' nephew, Goob, coming to town to beat some answers out of that poor night shift doctor. They arrested him for Assault and Battery, but he skipped bail and disappeared.

"So Goob Edgars is the long-lost nephew Effie mentioned?"

Noah nods and turns to the next page and reads for a few

moments. "What the hell, Cracker?" He gives a knowing shake of his head. "That old dog."

"What?"

"He just left it hanging. There's no more there in the book than he told us."

A tired waitress drops burgers in plastic baskets, teeming with greasy fries. "GThere you go," she says, leaving the check while she's at it. "Enjoy."

As they eat, Cheryl takes the book and checks the title page. "Crap, look at the copyright date. '1962.' He's slick as snot, isn't he? Stands there and blows smoke in my face and then sells me a book that's almost thirty years out of date."

"Hate to say, but that's Cracker for you."

"Now I feel bad dragging you around. I guess today was a waste of time for both of us."

"I'd kind of changed my mind about that part."

That surprises her, although she has been sensing more than just friendliness from him. Not necessarily a sexual vibe, but a warmth that is welcome after the cold shoulders and curious stares she's been getting.

"I guess I'd have to agree with that, Noah."

He wipes his mouth, then looks up and smiles at her. "You don't remember me at all, do you?"

Flustered, she says, "Remember you from . . .?"

"It's okay. I might not have recognized you either if I hadn't had such a big crush on you." His look turns teasing.

Looking directly into his eyes, she does find something that seems familiar, like that moment she first saw him on horseback, but she can't put it together. "Crush? From grade school?" she guesses.

He sits and waits.

Then, just like that, she remembers. "Oh my god, you . . . you were . . . in trouble all the time. You and another kid . . .who was that? With the lazy eye."

"You do remember. My partner in crime was Rudy."

She laughs. "That little rat cut in front of me in the cafeteria, so I shoved him, and then old lady Walters gave me swats."

"And I remember you gave Rudy a black eye."

Cheryl scoffs. "And I recall he turned into a ham actor, flopping around on the floor like an NBA star."

Noah laughs. "Randy was good at that sort of thing."

Now that Cheryl realizes who he is, she remembers him as the shy, bright one, always hanging on the fringes with the rougher Native kids, but not really with them. In their small school district, the Natives have always been somewhat apart. They're accepted in school, but there's not that much co-mingling.

Noah had been smart in class, even though she sensed even back then that he deliberately played it down. "I always thought you were the one who dreamed up the pranks, and Rudy got caught."

He grins. Well, I *was* the one who got him to cut in front of you."

"You dog. Really? I should've known." But his name isn't right, somehow. "We didn't call you Noah, though. I would've remembered that name."

"No, that's my middle name. Started using it after high school. My first name is Carroll, but if anyone ever made fun of that, the fight was on."

Cheryl laughs, remembering the teasing he got. "That's right. It wasn't spelled like a girl's name, though."

"No, it's C-A-R-R-O-L-L. A family name from my mother's side. I never heard the end of it from the other kids, though. Back then, they would call me Carroll and him Rudolph just to piss us off."

"Where is Rudy now?"

"Died in McAlester. Doing five years for robbery."

"You mean someone killed him in there?"

"No. AIDS." His face looks drawn as he remembers.

"I'm sorry. Were you still friends?"

"No, he went . . . went bad a long time ago. I couldn't . . . we had a falling out."

"That's tough."

They go back to their burgers. When she looks up again, Noah is staring at her. "I remember when you married Doyle. Always wondered why."

"That makes two of us. I was an idiot." She raises her eyebrows at him. "And who's the pretty woman in the wedding picture?"

"You wouldn't know her. I have no idea where she is now. She left me. Probably in jail."

"Any kids?" Cheryl asks.

"No. That would've gotten in the way of her drug habit." He says it with sadness rather than bitterness.

"So, what do you do out there on your farm?"

"Grow a few crops, do some leather work, take mountain guide gigs when I can get them. It's a solitary life. It suits me."

He's so easy going, she wonders if maybe he isn't a pothead himself. His house didn't have that lingering smell, though, that marijuana leaves. When they finish their lunch, Cheryl asks, "You mind if I pick up Josey first on the way to dropping you off?"

"No problem," he says.

A half hour later, they settle Josey in Cheryl's red pickup. The patient is scary to look at, her face a puffy red, one eye nearly swollen shut. Luckily, she is lightly sedated and has prescriptions to hasten the healing.

When they stop for the prescriptions, Cheryl heads to a pay phone and punches in Silas's number. She waits, tapping her foot as it rings. on the other end. Someone picks up the phone but doesn't speak. There is movement in the background.

"Silas? Hello?"

"This is Police Chief Bointy. Is this Cheryl?"

Her heart sinks. "Why are you there? Is Silas alright?"

CHAPTER SEVENTEEN

By the time Cheryl arrives with Noah and Josey, red and blue ambulance lights whirl in the coming darkness outside Silas's place. From somewhere in a back room, his Chihuahuas bark and howl at the invasion of their kingdom.

Paramedics have Silas strapped to a gurney and whisk him out the front door. As they head toward the waiting ambulance, Cheryl hurries over and walks alongside them. "What happened?"

The EMT's motion her off as they hustle him into the back of the ambulance. "Out of the way, ma'am. Please."

All Cheryl can see is his blood-smeared, swollen face. She grabs the porch rail to steady herself.

Noah grabs her elbow. "Hey, you better sit down."

They watch as Silas is loaded in. The ambulance siren wails as it takes off for Southwest Memorial.

"This is my fault," she tells Noah, sinking into a patio chair. Through the front door, she glimpses his ransacked living room, which looked eerily like Effie's.

After a few minutes, Chief Bointy and Shelby Myers come outside.

Bointy looks at Noah with surprise. "Noah," he says with a friendly head nod.

Noah asks, "How bad is he, Asa?"

Bointy shakes his head, clearly concerned. "He couldn't talk."

"I should never have left him alone." Cheryl struggles not to break down.

"You couldn't have known," Noah reassures her.

"He was the next obvious person. How could I not have known. Didn't anybody here report seeing anything?"

Shelby shakes his head, "I was out in the country with old man Biggs. Some coyotes got into his chicken shed."

"The Boney sisters called this in a half-hour ago," Bointy said. "What do you mean, he was the next obvious person?"

"I was going to tell you about it, first thing. I found out late last night that Silas was hiding a map for Effie."

"What's this?" Bointy asks.

"What kind of map?" Shelby asks.

"An old treasure map Effie asked him to safeguard."

Angry and frustrated, Bointy shakes his head. "And you didn't think that was information I need to know?"

"He only showed it to me and my lawyer last night. I was trying to check it out today."

Bointy nods toward Noah. "So that's why you got Pawnee boy here with you, huh?"

"I'm sorry, Chief," Cheryl says. "I was supposed to leave

it with Silas, but I brought it along so I could show it to him." She nods toward Noah. "Josey said . . . oh my god, Josey."

Turning, she sees Assistant Chief Myers guiding her lawyer toward the porch.

"Look who I found," Shelby says with a sympathetic smile.

Josey looks up at everyone, her swollen eye slits making her look like a punching bag. "What's happened to Uncle Silas?" she asks.

Bointy says, "He's hurt pretty bad. I got the boys comin' over from Lawton to work the scene. So far, no witnesses. Everybody on this street must be deaf not to hear the ruckus in there."

Cheryl pulls the map out of her purse and hands it to the Chief. "Here's what they were after."

"This is the map?" he asks.

"It's an old leather map Silas was keeping for Effie. It's connected to an old treasure."

"What?" Josey says sharply. "You had that with you? I can't believe it."

"I know you said not to," Cheryl says to Josey, "but I thought our guide should see the real thing."

Josey bristles. "So what did he say?"

"I told her it's a great museum piece, but we'll never find the treasure using it, unless you take a metal detector to all the

Wildlife Refuge."

"I'll be damned," Bointy mutters. "You're saying one person's dead and another beaten half to death over this? An old piece of leather, that's now worthless?"

Noah nods and shrugs. "In my not too humble opinion."

"Looks like whoever's after it is as stupid about this stuff as I am," Cheryl says.

Behind them, the barking Chihuahuas' howl crescendo to symphony levels. "Can somebody do something with those damn dogs?" Bointy asks. "They're in the middle of a crime scene."

No one jumps in with an offer, so Cheryl finally says, "I can keep them at my place for the night at least."

"Thanks, Cheryl," Bointy offers. "I think that qualifies you for triple points in heaven."

Cheryl gives Josey a dose of the medicine they prescribed for her and takes her to her R.V. to sit in the recliner in front of the TV. Noah helps her round up the four Chihuahuas into Cheryl's R.V. They promptly jump on Cheryl's bed and present such a fierce front that he mentally throws in the towel and lets them stay there.

She tells Noah, "I've got to go to the hospital, see about Silas, but I can drop you off first if you want."

"Mind if I tag along?" he asks. "Looks like you could use some company."

He's right. Cheryl really doesn't want to go by herself. She feels so guilty her stomach has hardened into a knot.

From the recliner, Josey sighs. "I'd love to go, but I'm so nauseous and exhausted, I don't think I can move."

"I'll give him a hug for you," Cheryl assures her. "Stay here and rest."

Twenty minutes later, as they find the nurse's desk on Silas's floor, they run into Dr. Hokeah, making notes on a chart.

"Hello again," Cheryl says. Off his blank look, she jolts his memory. "I brought in the poison oak victim earlier?"

"Oh, of course. Sorry, it's been a long day."

"We wanted to check on Mr. Weintraub. He's my neighbor."

"If you're not family--"

"I'm his contact person."

Hokeah flips through the chart. "Sure enough. So, Mr. Weintraub has multiple contusions and bruising. Blunt force trauma to the back of his head. He's stable.

Noah asks, "He hasn't been able to say who did this to him?"

The doctor shakes his head. "He's scheduled for a cat scan as soon as possible."

Cheryl tries to hold down the bile coming up her throat. Noah puts his hand on her arm He moves her to a bench.

Dr. Hokeah turns to them. "Best thing you could do is go home and get some rest."

She gets herself under control enough to speak. "Could I please just peek in on him for a second? Please?" Suddenly, if she can't hold his hand for a moment, she'll die.

"I guess it won't hurt. Just for a minute." He nods at the nurse, who gives them Silas's room number.

Cheryl and Noah walk into the whoosh of a breathing machine and the hum of lighted monitors that coil around his bed like an icy snake. Her knees nearly buckle at seeing him so helpless.

"Oh, Silas," she whispers, touching his hand. "I'm so sorry."

"Man," Noah says softly behind her. "They beat the shit out of him." He pats her shoulder. "I'll let you alone. Be right outside."

She sits by the bed and offers a prayer." Unlike people who find them superficial, she believes in trench prayers. When does anyone need a heavenly presence more? As much as she had strayed from organized religion, much to her mother's dismay, her upbringing always kicks in when things look grim.

A nurse enters and pulls the sheet up around his neck. "I'm afraid you'll need to go now."

"No, don't . . .,' Cheryl says.

"Sorry, the doctor said--"

"I meant the covers. He doesn't like anything close to his neck like that." Gently, Cheryl pulls the cover down a little.

"No problem." The nurse pats Cheryl's shoulder in

sympathy.

The ride to Noah's place is quiet, but the air carries the smells of damp earth and a hint of smoke, as though an unseen force was just beyond the next hill. On the radio Neil Young sings a plaintive song about the damage done.

CHAPTER EIGHTEEN

After hours of sitting on a cold, damp floor, every part of the woman's body feels bent and cramped. The plastic ties on her hands hold them so tightly her shoulders and arms are numb. But nothing is worse than the filthy gag pushed into her mouth.

The man has placed her against a structural column, her torso securely taped to it. Blindfolded, she only knows him by a funky smell, a blend of car mechanic and old sweat. She hears people moving above her.

Who took her? Suddenly, pounced on from behind as she got out of her car at the gym. Then a sweet, chemical smell. Then nothing. No clue what they want.

No one speaks to her. Occasionally, he cuts the duct tape and helps her to a tiny toilet. She feels him hovering in the open door as she tries to relax enough to relieve herself. She doesn't know how long it's been now, and she no longer trusts her sense of time.

She understands not to speak, even in a whisper. When she tried the first time, he removed the gag and slapped her hard enough to rattle her. It has been his only communication. She is a fast learner, she reminds herself. Stay alert. Anything might help. Yet with each passing hour, she grows more terrified that it will make no difference in the end.

CHAPTER NINETEEN

When Cheryl finally drags in home, she checks on Josey, who's asleep in the second bedroom. Trying not to make a sound, she retrieves the vodka bottle she keeps stashed under the sink and lets Silas's horde outside to do their business before calling it a night.

It will take her a few drinks to get to sleep tonight. She falls into one of her green plastic Adirondacks and unscrews the lid.

With the bottle almost to her lips, she has no idea what makes her pause. Perhaps it's the Chihuahuas, looking lost, wondering among themselves where Silas has gone. They probably don't get why their leashes aren't tied to Silas's lawn mower handles so he can walk them properly like he does every night.

The sharp acidic smell of the alcohol bristles in her nose. She studies the bottle, shame welling up inside. Staring up, she sees the moon is on the wane, allowing stars to jump out, almost silver against the indigo sky. Feral smells drift past from the small woods behind the mobile homes.

It would be easy to drink at her own sense of guilt, drink at the clients who are talking behind her back, at the law, who's got it so wrong. She knows that is a luxury that drunks cannot afford. Still, that voice in her head insists she needs it, even deserves it.

Then an image pops into Cheryl's head, of herself as a

girl, tormenting boys and climbing trees in the backyard of her childhood home in Medicine Wheel. She even recognizes her catalogue-ordered green-and-blue plaid seersucker shorts set.

The thought occurs to her, I never needed a drink then. It brings a tentative hope, even calm, that has been absent since Effie was killed. Cheryl had been happy as a child, never had to alter reality then. Why now?

Before she can talk herself out of it, she carries the vodka to the edge of the porch railing and dumps it out. "That's for you, Silas."

It feels good. Clean. A new resolve comes with it. No more, she tells herself. No more until Silas is . . .. But she sees the trap she's setting for herself and changes the thought to taking it by an hour at a time, each minute, if she has to.

She forces the Chihuahuas to make room for her on her own bed. When she crawls under the covers, they make her giggle as they cuddle next to her on top of the blanket. Their warm, tiny bodies help her sleep most of the night.

The next morning, Cheryl is pulled awake by Josey's voice, talking low over the phone.

"Okay, Shelby, thanks. See you later." She turns to Cheryl. "Good morning. You slept in."

Cheryl checks the clock. "Jees, after eight. That's late for me."

"I did manage to find coffee," Josey says.

Cheryl is impressed, especially given the lawyer's still swollen eyes and blotchy face. "Looks like your puffiness has gone down a bit."

"I'm still on the relaxants, but yeah."

"You talking to Shelby Myers?"

"Yeah, he's run into a dead end with Goob, the prospector's nephew. The files were lost in a jail flood years ago."

"Oh, brother," Cheryl moans. "If the law doesn't have any record . . .." Then it hits her. "You know what? The library has a microfilm section. I could look up old newspaper stories."

"Don't you have jobs for today?" Josey asks.

"Normally, I would, but that's dried up overnight. I'm a pariah now."

Outside, the Lawrence's BMW purrs to a stop in front of Cheryl's place.

"Oh, crap." Cheryl heads to the door.

Katie Lawrence smooths her pants suit and pushes up her bouffant as she exits the car. When Cheryl opens the door, Katie says, "I need to talk to you." Her tone is business cool. "Is Silas's niece here with you?"

Cheryl stalls her with, "Yeah, just let me make sure she's decent."

She hurries inside and tells Josey, "She's either here to pry or gloat. Don't tell her anything." Then she opens the door.

"This is Katie Lawrence," Cheryl says, "And this is my lawyer, Josey Spangler."

Katie suppresses a gasp when she sees Josey's swollen, erupted face. She not only looks hesitant to touch her but acts as though she is loath to touch anything in the living room. She doesn't even sit down.

"This won't take a second," Katie assures them. "Cliff wanted me to let you know how badly we both feel about Silas. He was so special to Effie." Then she segues to the real point of her visit.

"Cheryl, Cliff found a new codicil to Effie's will."

"Really?" Cheryl manages, her face reddening. "Just popped up?"

"In our safe deposit box, actually. Effie gave it to Cliff for safekeeping. He just hadn't realized what it was until he got into it yesterday."

Josey pulls herself up. "May I see it? I represent Ms. Jackson now."

"That was another reason I dropped by," Katie says coolly. "To set up a formal reading of the document."

Josey doesn't skip a beat. "The sooner the better."

Cheryl opens the door to let her out.

Holding her ground, Katie says, "We're going out to the cabin this weekend, check on the new pool, but right after that?"

"We'll give Cliff a call." Cheryl opens the door a little wider.

Katie purses her lips like a cobra. "Fine. We just didn't

want you to be taking out any loans against something that may not pan out. Bye now. See you soon."

Cheryl closes the door and turns to Josey. "So that's it. Cliff and Katie are overextended at the bank. What do you bet they've taken out loans against every penny they thought they had coming from Effie? That's where that new swimming pool is coming from."

"You think they killed Miss Lawrence for it?"

Cheryl shakes her head. "They'd never get their own hands dirty."

"Hey, you know what? I've got a friend at the Credit Bureau who could check their credit rating."

"Really?"

"I'll get right on it."

"Good. I'll head to the Lawton library then. See if I can locate a picture of Goob Edgars.

An hour later, feeling energized, Cheryl sits in a cubicle in the Lawton Public Library, turning the knob on a microfiche machine as black and white images whoosh by. She plows through the Lawton Constitution stories from 1938 and 39 before she finally gets a hit.

The headline from May 4, 1940, reads, *Doctor Assaulted in Hospital.* Below that, a picture of the doctor in a bloodied white lab coat, being loaded on a stretcher into an ambulance.

She reads the article, muttering to herself. "*Attacked with a knife by Goob Edgars . . . related to doctor's treatment of a patient, according to hospital personnel. Yes. The suspect got away . . . . Wow."*

From behind her comes a voice. "No talking to yourself in the library." Cheryl nearly jumps out of her seat.

Noah stands there grinning at her.

"You scared me half to death," she laughs. "What are you doing, stalking me?"

"Researching buried loot in the area. Like we talked about yesterday."

"Find anything?"

He holds up three large books. "A few things to check out. I thought that looked like your truck out front."

"I found an article on Edgar's nephew beating up the doctor, but no pictures of him so far."

"Do they keep mug shots that old at the Police Department?"

"Usually, but all those records got lost in a flood."

"That's too bad. Listen, I was going to drop by and see you later. Been asking around a little more. I may have a couple of tidbits for you. Wanna have coffee in a bit?" They plan to meet at the Big Chief in a couple of hours.

After a few minutes, something catches her eye. She flips back to the headline: *Attacker skips bail, flees.* She scans the story and finds, *"Goob Edgars."* With pictures inside. "Alright! Yes, yes, yes."

The small mug shot of the accused is grainy black-and-white. A dark-haired thin man with an angular face, cheekbones jutting out, eyes a little wild. He doesn't resemble anyone she knows.

Cheryl rolls the knob to move to the inside story on the screen. Suddenly, she senses a presence behind her in the stacks. The hair on the back of her neck shivers and stands up.

Then footsteps clap against the wooden floor, rushing toward her like an animal attacking from the rear. As she starts to turn around, a sharp crack to her head echoes in the hollows of the library.

CHAPTER TWENTY

Someone shakes her shoulders. "Cheryl? Wake up, Cheryl."

When she opens her eyes, the frightened face of the librarian flutters above her. Cheryl knows her, Joan Cooley, a Medicine Wheel local who works in Lawton.

"Cheryl, are . . . ?"

Behind Joan, Josey's puffy face hovers, pale and concerned. The microfilm files lay scattered on the floor and the machine smashed.

"Should we call an ambulance?" Cooley frets, then decides, "I'd better. Or else somebody'll sue." She looks sadly at the ruined microfiche machine. "And will you just look what they did?"

"No ambulance," Cheryl says through a haze, though she's in no condition to make that judgment.

"I'll drive her to the hospital, get her checked out," Josey says.

The librarian hesitates. "Someone needs to look at her."

"It's okay," Josey insists, then looks closely at Cheryl. "Is that what you want?"

"I guess," Cheryl says, but she has no idea what she

wants.

They get to Josey's Camry and Cheryl gives her directions. As they ride into Lawton, Cheryl thinks to ask, "Why were you there? In the library?"

"I couldn't wait to tell you . . . my friend at Credit Union worked quick." She leans in close and whispers. "You were so right. Cliff and Katie are up to their eyeballs in debt."

Despite her headache, Cheryl manages to smile. "I knew it."

"I just jumped in the car and came to find you." Josey looks over at her. "Could you see who did it? Did you see anything?"

"Came out of nowhere." Cheryl shakes her head.

"The librarian said no one saw anybody, either."

When they reach the Southwest Medical Center, Dr. Hokeah, who treated Josey the day before, looks Cheryl over in a room just off the Emergency area.

"Do you know what hit you?" Hokeah asks, examining the egg already cropping up on her skull.

Cheryl shakes her head. "I just heard footsteps and then everything went black."

He records some notes. "You got a hard whack, whatever it was. We better do a cat scan."

"I can't do that."

He looks at her, puzzled. "A cat scan will give us a better

idea of what's going on, Miss Jackson."

She's too embarrassed to tell him she has no health insurance. After the wreck that nearly cost her a leg, no private company has ever talked to her. She's eligible for the state's insurance pool, but her monthly premium would amount to two thirds of her usual income.

"It's a painless procedure," he says with a smile. "We can give you a relaxant before the scan, if that's it."

"No. I don't want to. Period." Her too forceful answer makes her cringe inside. *It isn't the doctor's fault*, she chides herself. "I'm sorry. The fact of the matter is I don't have insurance and I can't afford to have it done, okay? Can't you just treat me like you would have before cat scans came along?"

He regards Cheryl with respect. "I appreciate your candor. And, since you appear to be hard-headed in several areas . . . well, don't be by yourself, alright?"

"I won't let her out of my sight. We'll be fine," Josey offers, seemingly unaware that she herself resembles a radiation victim.

Hokeam shakes his head with a gallows humor grin. "You're both walking wounded. Watch each other's backs."

"If anything happens with your vision, like blurring, seeing double—anything at all, I want you back here? Got it?"

Cheryl looks in on Silas for a minute before they leave. He looks to her as if he's part of some hideous experiment, gnarled in white sheets and plastic tubing. His usual ruddy complexion is pale as dough, and looks almost detached, like a rubber face mask.

His niece seems lost for words. They both stand at his bedside for a few minutes, Cheryl saying a little prayer and squeezing his hand. She sees above his hospital band the numbers tattooed into his forearm so many decades ago. *Just come back to us, Silas. It's not your time yet. You didn't survive Auschwitz to go out like this.*

On the drive back from Lawton to Medicine Wheel, it comes back to Cheryl where she was in her research when somebody bonked her from behind. She looks to Josey. "Did you see what I found in the microfiche? The picture of Goob Edgars?"

She shakes her head. "No. The machine was smashed to bits. You mean you found a photograph of him?"

"It was his mug shot," Cheryl says in frustration. "Real hard to see, but I was about to read the story when this happened."

"You were on to something, Cheryl. That's all there is to it. And somebody knew it. We've got to talk to the Police Chief."

CHAPTER TWENTY-ONE

By the time Cheryl and Josey walk into Medicine Wheel Police Station a half hour later, Cheryl has started to see double. It comes and goes, but as Josey reports the assault to Chief Bointy and Assistant Chief Myers, her lawyer sometimes morphs into two people.

Josey is appropriately indignant about the accused conspirator being the one who got knocked out, reminding the lawmen that they have charged the wrong person. She doesn't leave out a detail, including that the doctor wanted more tests than Cheryl could afford.

It's clear that the police chief is concerned. He has known her since she was a teenager and always treated her right. What Cheryl also notices is that he resents Silas's niece rolling into town, self-righteous and accusatory. Cheryl knows Bointy would rather feed a bear raw steak with his fingers than deal with lawyers.

Apparently unaware of that, Josey works up steam. Even her swollen eyes water up. "So, what do you think of your arrest of my client now, huh? Now that people are running her down in public libraries while she's trying to do the research you all should be doing."

"Now just hold your horses," Bointy holds his thick hands up in a calming gesture. "It so happens we *have* been doing due diligence on Goob Edgars." He nods toward Shelby, who hovers over his computer just across the aisle, unabashedly eavesdropping. "Shelby?"

Shelby clears his throat then begins in an official voice. "We found out that since Edgars' nephew skipped bail here, he's been spotted over the years in Arizona and New Mexico, and even back in this region, but never arrested. Last time anybody reported seeing him was in 1948. And the trail ends there. He just disappeared."

Bointy shifts his unlit cigar stub from one side of his mouth to the other, enjoying that his Assistant just brought Josey's indignation down a notch.

Cheryl squints her eyes to make the two images of Bointy merge into one. "Isn't there some kind of national directory you could run his name through? I found a picture that was awful grainy on the microfilm. Don't know if anyone could identify him from it.

Bointy leans back in his chair. "You think we haven't? We're not quite the hillbillies your lawyer thinks. Everything came back empty. Maybe he changed his name. Or maybe he gave up the outlaw trail." He looks over to Shelby. "How old did you say he'd be now?"

Shelby brightens at being brought into the conversation again. He barely glances at a paper. "Seventy."

"So he could still be out there," Bointy allows. "You find that background on Mrs. Lawrence yet?"

Eager to please, Shelby is already reading from the files as he joins them. "Married in Las Vegas, 1947. To Ben Lawrence. That's Cliff's uncle. Her maiden name, interestingly enough, was left blank on the marriage certificate."

"Only in Vegas, huh?" Bointy cracks.

"Her name as the nurse wasn't in the microfiche article about the doctor getting beaten, either," Cheryl says, trying to subtly cover one eye so she only sees a single image. "I thought that was odd."

"Law enforcement blacked out the names of the people who treated old Charlie Edgars," Bointy says. "I remember someone telling me about that. They could do that kind of thing back then. After the doctor was attacked, they weren't going to risk anybody else getting beaten half to death because they worked a shift in the hospital."

"Where are those original files?" Josey asks.

"Long gone, lost in a basement flood." Shelby turns a page. "Effie got married in '47, but it doesn't say when she left the clinic. Or what happened to her husband."

"I never heard her talk about him, not once," Cheryl says. "But I know she was an Army nurse during the war."

Bointy jumps in. "She disappeared for several years after it happened. Part of that time we know she was in Europe serving her country. The husband was kind of worthless, from what I've heard. Some locals assume he was killed in Korea. But we got his military records, and that wasn't the case. You got that, Shelby?"

"Right here," Shelby says. He was in the military, alright. Stationed right here at Ft. Sill. But he went AWOL in '56. Never heard from again."

"This is all well and good," Josey says, her indignation surfacing again, "but what about Cheryl getting attacked in the library? Will you be contacting the Lawton Police?"

Bointy sighs as though he's striving for patience. "Rest assured I will put it on the front burner."

Cheryl's head is swimming with double images and facts by the time she and Josey leave. It isn't until they get to their cars that Cheryl remembers where she was supposed to be. "Oh, no, I forgot to meet Noah. Drop me off at my pickup at the library. I'll see you at home later, okay?"

Then she remembers, Noah was there just before it happened. That makes her head hurt even more.

CHAPTER TWENTY-TWO

Keeping one eye closed as she drives over, Cheryl pulls in front of the Big Chief diner. She decides on the way that he won't be there if he was her attacker. Of course, she's so late he probably gave up on her and left, anyway.

Walking in, she looks around and doesn't see him. Then, from a table in the back, Noah waves, and shakes his head at her lateness.

"I'm so sorry," she says, hurrying to his table. "You're not going to believe what happened."

"It had better be good. After a whole pot of coffee, my head feels like a pinball machine.

"Then we're both in the same boat. I got hit with a baseball bat in the back of the head at the library."

He looks at her with alarm. "What? Who hit you?"

"Don't know." Cheryl detects nothing fishy from him and relays the details, except for the seeing double part. When she's finished, he leans back.

"You really okay? You look pale."

She turns so he can feel the back of her head. "Feel my egg?" She guides his fingers to the lump that has puffed up. Then she is embarrassed. She isn't sure why. "You didn't see anybody suspicious, I guess, when you were leaving."

"No. Wish I've been there when it happened. That's a helluva conk. Have you got somebody who can stay with you tonight? To check on you?"

"Josey. The blind leading the blind, I'm afraid."

"Have you eaten today?" Noah looks worried.

Cheryl comes up blank. Her stomach has been jittery for so many days, she seesaws back and forth between being too nauseous to eat, or stuffing herself on the go, followed by miserable indigestion.

Noah waves the waitress over. "What do you want?" he asks Cheryl.

"Our special today's Fish Tacos," the waitress suggests.

"Fine." Cheryl hopes it won't be too acidic, then remembers their fish is more breading than meat, so it will even out.

"And bring us some chips while we're waiting?" Noah asks the waitress.

For the first time that day, Cheryl finds herself relaxing a little. Even being nervous about her double vision, she feels comfortable with Noah, the way he's concerned but doesn't pry. He has an easiness about him, the kind that seems to elude her.

"Okay, so what did you find out?" she asks.

"Well, I'm willing to bet Cracker know more than he's saying. And Gray Bear, one of Bointy's old vet buddies, says the

James loot has already been dug up."

"What? Then what . . . oh Lord, I'm confused."

"It came from Gray Bear's father. First time I'd heard that from a reliable source. Not sure what to think."

"But Effie guarded that map from the moment she got it 50 years ago."

"I know. So maybe somebody else got a look at it? Without her knowing? Where'd she keep it?"

"In her safe deposit box for years, but Silas says she got paranoid after Cliff found out, probably through his Uncle Ben. Effie never trusted Cliff. She took it out of there and hid it in the walls of her mobile home."

After a moment, she asks, "How do the Natives know about the James treasure, anyway?"

"They say that old man Cracker—Cracker's dad—had some antique coins after the old prospector died. Old Cracker had Indian blood and knew them all back then. The elders say those coins came from Edgars' cache."

"But if the old man did find it, why not just say it?"

Noah tipped his head. "Think about it. Ownership and taxes alone would make him wary. Plus, those James boys had lots of friends, not to mention kinfolks, who were anxious for a finger in that pie, legal or not."

The waitress shows up with food and coffee. Cheryl realizes her headache is easing off. "But if old Cracker somehow found all that money, why is his son running a dirty, dilapidated junk store?"

"Good point. But I also would ask if maybe Miss Lawrence was handier with a shovel than she let on?"

Cheryl laughs. "All a hundred pounds of her? No. Effie was a strict Bible thumper. She called it filthy lucre from the James brothers' sins.

"Then someone else had to have seen that map. Any possibility it was Silas?"

"No, he didn't come here until the 60's. He and his sister survived Auschwitz. She lived in Tulsa with her American husband and convinced Silas to come over."

"I never knew that." Noah stares through the diner's window. "What about Effie's husband then?"

"He went AWOL from Ft. Sill in the mid-fifties. He could have found it, cashed in the coins and took off."

"I wonder where we can get a look at his military record. Maybe the Army knows."

"I can check with some friends at the base."

Hopeful, Cheryl looks up at him. "Does that mean you want to keep working on this?"

He shrugs and grins. "I am beyond curious now."

She feels a huge sense of relief. Just to connect with someone so knowledgeable gives her a boost.

"I've been reading that book I bought. This area has the wildest history."

"Yep, outlaw gangs from all over crisscrossed back and forth through here."

As she eats, he talks about not only the James brothers, but the Youngers, the Doolin gang, and the Daltons, riding their escape routes and burying their spoils, back in wide open Indian Territory.

By the time they finish, Cheryl is surprised that it's nearly dark. "I better get home. It's so much fun listening to you tell these stories. Thanks."

Noah gives her arm a little tug as he sees her out to her truck. "You take care now. I can tell from the way you're squinting your eyes that your vision is off. Or something. Watch that head."

He waves as he walks away, then pauses and turns back. "Listen, you've got my number. You call me, any time, day or night. Okay?"

CHAPTER TWENTY-THREE

Cheryl sits in the truck watching Noah walk to his own pickup—actually, two of him—with a sense of calm that she hasn't felt all week. No trembles in the stomach. No shaky hands. And, miraculously, she doesn't want a drink.

Driving down the twisting streets of Medicine Wheel, with their natural cobblestone buildings, the wide ancient creek flowing through the middle of town, Cheryl thinks about how much she loves this place, even if it is riddled with contradictions. Built over a natural hot springs and river that Native ancestors considered sacred healing waters, an undertow of shame also resides here, as throughout Oklahoma.

When white men wrote their history, they shielded their offspring from the cruel details of their treatment of the Natives. As if the relocation of the tribes into Indian Territory had not been harsh enough, the government heaped on more misery with short rations, rancid meat, and treaties that proved to be jokes. The poisonous side of manifest destiny.

Sometimes Cheryl wonders how she can love this state so much, with its startlingly corrupt politicians, its penchant for high incarceration rates and executions. A place where almost half of the population goes to church more than once a week, yet white supremacist communities and meth labs thrive.

Still, if she was in the trenches, down and out, there is no one she would rather have beside her than an Okie. There's something about pioneer stock that knows how to come through. People even smile and greet strangers on the street just because it often feels like the right thing to do.

By the time she drives past Cracker's General Store, she has nearly forgotten her plan to go inside. But she's caught a second wind. And the store light is still on, so she pulls in at the end of the block and walks back up the street toward the entrance.

Before she gets there, she hears Cracker's rusty voice cut into the still night air. The place is devoid of customers. When she peeks through the storefront window, she sees him in double circles, talking on the phone by the cash register. Something dark in his tone pushes her back into the shadows to listen.

"Because I'm takin' most of the risk on this end, you know. And with everything that's happened, I don't like the direction this is headed. Doesn't seem to me you're getting jack done on your end . . . Well, see that you do. Or I'll dump the whole damn thing. And I'm not whistlin' Dixie."

Cheryl peeks a moment as he slams down the phone and takes a long drag of his cigarette before stubbing it out. After a moment, his boots click on the hardwood floor as he huffs to the entrance and turns the *OPEN* sign to *CLOSED*. As he shuts the blinds, she ducks back and steps on a dead catalpa branch.

Hearing the crunch, he goes still, then slowly turns in her direction. Her heart pounds so loud it seems he can surely hear it from inside the store. She stays frozen in the darkness for what feels like minutes but is probably much less. Then, finally, she hears him walk toward the stairs and start down.

As his voice fades, she hears him say, "You damn dogs

shut up now."

Cheryl hurries back to her pickup and sits hunched over the wheel, breathing hard. She tries to control a growing sense of panic. Then, suddenly, she wants a drink so bad she can barely swallow.

The hotel and bar are only blocks away. No doubt, however, she would probably run into Doyle. That gives her pause. Right now, she would rather go head-to-head with a rattlesnake than talk to him about whatever it was they did the night Effie was murdered.

She concentrates on saying things from A.A. *The urge will pass. Do something else. Do anything else. Where are you going to be five minutes after you take that drink?*

Then, as though the universe opens to her, she knows what she needs to do. She puts the pickup in gear, slides in an Amy LaVere CD full blast, and heads to Lawton. She has to close one eye to see the right number of highway lines, but that's okay. If this doesn't go away, I'm going to have to get a patch, she thinks. *Great, run around looking like a pirate.*

Cheryl rolls down her window and lets the cold air blow on her face. It smells of loam and asphalt, and feral creatures roaming the night. She wonders if the wildlife in the Refuge are restless tonight, too. The panic for a drink fades a bit. Making it to the hospital in twenty minutes, she slips past the vacant nurses' station.

Silas looks the same, except his puffy face has gone down some. The breathing machine is gone, along with its unnerving whoosh, rising and falling. She holds his hand and tries to send him what she hopes is healing energy.

"It's me, Silas. It's Cheryl. I sure miss you, buddy. The dogs are fine but can't figure out where you are. Oh, and Pretty Boy tried to take a bite out of Katie today. You would have loved it."

It feels odd talking to him without his cutting her off before she finishes a sentence. "Not a lot of news. Or developments. I haven't got much work to do. Suddenly, nobody needs me to do anything. They don't come right out with it, but I get the message."

She strokes his hand. "Sorry, everything seems so trivial beside what you're going through. If only you were awake to tell us . . . anything. Like, if you dug up some of that treasure, after all?" Cheryl sits there for a long time, until she hears herself humming lullabies.

CHAPTER TWENTY-FOUR

The woman can feel her strength ebbing with each passing hour. Fear has paralyzed everything she usually relies on—courage, smarts, self-confidence. The stale, oily odors that make her think of a garage have dulled her.

She's not giving up—not by a long shot—but if there is any chance to get free, it will have to be soon. If not, she might be too weak to take advantage of it.

It amazes her how dehumanizing tying one's hands behind the back feels. Every part of her feels splayed open, vulnerable--face, heart, stomach. Then taped up, blindfolded, your back to a pole and to have to sit there, legs spread-eagled, makes her think she's bait. Especially when the dogs wander in and sniff her up and down.

She tries to remember that she is strong and fast. Hours of playing tennis and doing weights at the gym will serve her well. If only she could find an opening.

His heavy footsteps announce his presence, and she is grateful. He has made her wait to relieve herself much longer than usual, although her sense of time has deteriorated to such an extent that she can't even be sure of that. He takes out her gag, frees her numb hands and unties her from the column.

She sits gratefully on the toilet seat, sensing, as always, his presence in the doorframe, watching. All of a sudden, the dogs who have mingled around her the past few days, start barking, close up and with an intensity that scares her. She thinks they are running away from her direction, then hears them howling from another room.

Her captor mumbles, "What the fuck?" The first words she's heard out of his mouth. He moves away from the doorway. Then his steps retreat.

The woman yanks down her blindfold and blinks into the dim light of a filthy utility bathroom, where some small, abandoned motors have been stashed on the floor.

The man is gone. This is her chance. She bolts off the toilet and tries to get her bearings. It looks like a pack rat's place, all dusty shelves overflowing with junk. Panting, she sees to one side the tiny area where he held her. It leads to another room, bigger and even junkier. She sees double stairs lead up toward a swallowing darkness.

She hurries toward them, willing her stiff legs to move, grateful for the dogs barking to cover the noise. As she reaches the stairs, she hears him yelling at the dogs from another room. They yelp as he strikes them.

"Settle down, damn it," he screams.

Moving up the stairs in near darkness, she senses entering a larger space. As her eyes adjust, she makes out the faint glow of a distant street light filtering through a door that leads outside.

She runs into something on the floor—*is that a wooden Indian?* Then his footsteps clack from behind her as he comes up the stairs for her.

Tripping over something else, the pain causes her to cry out. *Just get to the door.* And, somehow, she does. There's even a car coming up the street, its headlights flashing on the building.

The woman screams for help while she struggles with the door latch.

His enormous hand clamps around her mouth. He wraps his other arm around her waist and yanks her out of sight.

She jabs an elbow in his face and hears him grunt at the contact, but he doesn't let go. She can barely make out his face in the dark but knows it makes no difference. Now he will kill her. That is the last thing she thinks as his fist slams into her jaw and she sees stars.

Later, when she comes to, she's still in the big room upstairs, but tied up and gagged. She hears him talking on the phone.

"No, you've got to fix it now. Not me, I can't do that. I've done everything else, but I will not do that."

The woman tries to stay conscious, but everything blurs again, and she passes out. A few minutes later he rolls her up in a canvas drop cloth.

CHAPTER TWENTY-FIVE

The next morning Cheryl takes a deep breath to fortify herself before pushing open Pioneer Bank's entrance door. She has on a black eye patch Silas wore following eye surgery, but she still feels like a cheesy pirate act. It has become too exhausting trying to keep one eye shut, which is the only way she can avoid seeing double.

At least she hasn't aggravated the vision problem with alcohol. Having notched another day without a drink, she's decided to go for Day Three. Her business at the bank promises to be the prissiest little task of the day, so she decides to get it out of the way first.

Cheryl approaches the only visible bank officer sitting at a desk, all the while cursing herself for not having introduced herself properly before. Silas has always told her she needs to have a banker who knows her by sight.

The young man squints as if he recognizes her but can't quite come up with the name. "Good morning, ma'am."

"Hi, I'm Cheryl Jackson, Mr.--" She looks at his desk plaque. "Smith."

"Yes, ma'am. Reeder Smith. How can I be of service?" She overlooks his fawning hospitality.

"It's regarding a payment on my truck."

"Certainly. Please, have a seat." He takes her information and disappears into the main office, returning after a few minutes with a folder. "Pertaining to the red Toyota?"

"That's it. The payment is due next week. I'm not going to be able to make it."

Mr. Martin's thin smile shifts to studied neutrality. "And what seems to be the problem, Miss Jackson?"

Her laugh is self-conscious. "Not enough money?" Her levity is lost on him. "Sorry, I didn't mean not to take it seriously," she quickly adds. But I am in a bit of a cash flow bind now."

He listens poker-faced then continues in a cool, noncommittal tone. "And exactly what is it you want the bank to do about it?"

"I thought if I came in and explained the problem, you might grant me an extension or something, I guess."

Reeder studies the file with a concerned frown. "Oh, I see. It appears the last several payments were made by Mrs. Lawrence."

"Yes, the one who left me her estate in her will."

"And was murdered last week." His look is so cold it gives her a shudder. Of course, she realizes, he knew who she was the second she walked in.

Cheryl feels herself rumble with anger yet tries to stay cool. It's hard not to stomp out. When and if she does see any money, this fat Ken doll can kiss her sweet ass.

That's what she's thinking as she shoves the bank door open, just as Doyle is reaching for the same handle to enter. The door frame smashes right into his nose.

"What the . . .." His nose immediately spurts blood.

"Oh my god," Cheryl exclaims, "I'm so sorry."

He is too stunned to do anything but step back, off balance and dazed.

"Here," she says, motioning to a sidewalk bench near the door. "Sit down."

"What the hell? You going to kill me now?"

"No, no, no, I was—I didn't even look in front of me. She fishes in her purse and finds some crumpled tissues. "Here, you're bleeding."

Doyle feels around the edges of his beautifully sculpted nose. "Damn right. You broke it," he whines, as if realizing it for the first time. "You broke my nose.

"I'm really sorry," Cheryl hates how much she has to say that. She want, needs to apologize, but another part of her also wants to say, *Oh, don't be such a little bitch.*

But Doyle is far from done. "Every time I run into you, it ends up like this. Me getting the raw end."

She reddens, remembering the night Effie died. "Is that what it was last Saturday night?" Cheryl says it more out of anger than inquiry, but the questioning look he shoots back surprises her.

He forgets about his nose long enough to smirk. "Yeah. Another dead end. Remember?"

Actually, she doesn't. But she knows him well enough to wait. He'll jump back in like he always does.

When he does, his voice is swimming somewhere in his adenoids. "What a bitch. I buy you drinks and you're all, *yeah, let's go*. Then by the time I get you in bed . . . well, you know the rest."

Again, she forces herself to wait him out. *Hold on. He'll get there.*

He does. "But *you* passing out on *me*?" He scoffs. "That's a good one."

Tears of relief leap up her throat. She wants to throw herself on him and scream her thanks, but she manages the wherewithal to ask, "So you've told the Chief everything you remember about that night?"

He snaps back at her. "Yeah. Which is practically nothing. I was drunk, too, remember?"

She puts her head in her hands as relief washes over her. *Why didn't you just ask him right away instead of torturing yourself all this time?* Cheryl knows the answer. *Because you think you deserve to suffer.* When she first heard that in a meeting, she loathed its prickly feel of truth. But she came to understand that while she hated being miserable, it was at least familiar territory. She was used to beating herself up, putting herself down, never being enough. Not even being okay.

For a moment, the truth is like a sweet waterfall. Now,

Doyle seems so small to her, there on the bench, with his bent shoulders and bloody face. "I am really sorry about your nose, Doyle."

"Well, you should be."

"Do you want me to take you to Dr. Hokeah? I'll be glad to."

He swells with indignation. "No. You've done enough." Doyle seems to notice her eyepatch for the first time. "What's with the pirate look?"

"Don't worry about it." Cheryl leaves, then hears him calling to her all the way down the block.

"I'm going to send you the bill."

Smiling, she waves at him without looking back. And she decides it's time to tackle the next task on her list, something that seemed too abhorrent to consider only minutes earlier: Find Cliff Lawrence.

CHAPTER TWENTY-SIX

Heading his cruiser toward Cracker's store, Asa Bointy is wondering what has happened to his sleepy little town. So close to his retirement, he had expected to ride it out easy. He's let himself go physically, which cost him plenty in new Triple-X uniforms. But who could predict all hell would break loose in the space of a week.

Up to his eyeballs in Effie's murder, now he has to chase down some phone messages that reported a disturbance at Cracker's store after midnight.

Maybe a fight, or even a robbery was the gist of the messages. As if the old fart has anything worth stealing.

Bointy knows for a fact that Cracker has a sawed-off hidden under his cash register, so if this was a robbery, he could be walking into the perpetrator's fresh corpse. When he pulls up, the *CLOSED* sign is on the front door.

He puts on his uniform hat, checks his gun, and heads toward the door. He raps several times before giving up and going around toward the back.

Cracker is putting a trash bag in his alley dumpster when Bointy sees him from the back.

"Morning, Cracker," the Chief says.

Cracker whirls around, nervous as a cat. When he sees

Cracker's face he can understand why. His jaw is swollen and bruised, puffed up almost to his eyes.

"Hey," Bointy says, "what happened to you?"

Cracker shakes his head. "I fell last night in the dark and my bedpost took a swing at me. Can you believe it?" He grins as best he can at his joke. After a moment of silence, he asks, "What brings you out?"

"Got a couple of calls on the machine this morning about noise over here during the night. Dogs raising a ruckus. Someone thought they heard screams."

"I was trying to take care of that when this happened." Cracker points to his face then heads toward the back entrance to the store. "Come on in. It stinks out here. You want a cup of coffee?"

"Don't mind if I do." Bointy follows him inside, where he smells it fresh brewing. "Aren't you open today?"

"Oh, yeah," Cracker says. "Just taking my sweet time with it. My face was swelled up like a water bag when I woke up. Trying to get myself together."

Bointy doesn't see anything that looks strange inside but also wonders why Cracker hasn't directly answered him about the reports. Living on the upper floor of the building, Cracker would hear any disturbance.

"So . . . anything out of the ordinary last night?"

Cracker hands him a cup of coffee. "Just the damn dogs. Must have been a skunk or a coon around.

Bointy sits down in a dusty chair opposite Cracker near the register. "What about somebody screaming?"

Cracker shrugs his shoulders. "Could've been the dogs. I gave them *what for*. Them dogs know better than to howl in a pack like that. They're my hunting dogs."

Bointy says. "Mmm . . . good coffee."

"I put in a tablespoon for every cup and then one for the pot." Cracker smiles and unlocks the front door.

Bointy can't put his finger on exactly what's off about Cracker. A little more hyper than usual, the way he doesn't want to look him in the eye? But he doesn't press.

"Well, alrighty then." Bointy finishes his cup and rises to leave. "Just wanted to check on you."

"I appreciate it, Chief." Cracker fiddles with opening his register.

As he heads toward the door. Bointy notices that the constantly dirty floor has a path leading toward the stairs that appears freshly mopped.

It seems odd, but then, Bointy thinks, *that's Cracker for you*. Hardly housekeeper of the year.

CHAPTER TWENTY-SEVEN

Business is dead at the John Deere store. Even Astrid, the perennial clerk-bookkeeper-manager, looks grateful for some activity when the bell on the entrance door sounds Cheryl's arrival.

"Morning, Cheryl." Astrid smooths the front her metallic blue caftan as she comes into the sales area. "You need a tractor?"

"Yeah, I want one of those new ones with the air-conditioned cabs. Cliff around?"

"Nope, he's off for a few days unless I need him. And I won't, trust me." Everyone knows Astrid really runs the place. Her only bad days are when Cliff decides to stick his nose in.

"Where's he at?"

"Remodeling the cabin."

"Oh, that's right."

"Yeah, they're talking about moving out there permanent . . . so Katie says she wants to get it just the way she wants it." Her side grin to Cheryl is as good as an eye roll.

Cheryl has to hand it to the Lawrences. They have more gall than anyone she knows. First, Cliff and Katie not only managed to "buy" Effie's place, without ever making a single payment over the years, according to Effie. Now they're moving ahead with their remodel, counting on Effie's estate to pay that off.

She can't let herself get in a stew about that, though, she knows. Self-righteous anger is a trigger for drunks, so Cheryl doesn't let herself go there. "Another makeover, huh? What are they doing now?"

Astrid looks around as if to check for possible spies. "I saw the invoice for their new hot tub."

Cheryl tries to sound only mildly interested. "Oh?"

"Mm hunh" She clicks her teeth. "Ten thousand."

A high-pitched sound escapes Cheryl's throat, somewhere between disgust and surprise.

"And, of course, you know they're digging ground for that new swimming pool in back of the place."

Cheryl nods, but, in fact, knows very little about what they're doing. "Okay, well, thanks, Astrid."

"What's with the eye patch, anyway?"

Cheryl gives her the rundown of the library attack. "It's driving me crazy, but if I keep both eyes open, I see double. It's kinda scary if you want to know the truth. And this eyepatch doesn't fit right. Gives me a headache."

"You've come to the right place."

"What?"

Astrid goes into her office and searches through the desk

drawers. "I had eye surgery a couple of years back. . .."

"I remember that. Pretty serious, wasn't it?"

"Lord, woman, they took my eyeball clean out of my head and fiddled around with my retina and then put it back in. I'm good as new now, but I—ah, here they are."

Astrid blows dust off a couple of eye patches, one black sequined and the other red satin.

"Good Lord-a-mighty." Cheryl laughs as she sees them. "Nothing plain for you."

Ten minutes later, the black sequined patch over one eye, she climbs into her truck, hoping not to run into anyone. *How do I explain worn-out jeans, t-shirt, baseball cap and a smudge of sequins over my eye?* But it does make her smile.

On the way back home, she drives past many of her former clients' mobile homes. She knows without looking that some have parted a slit in the curtains to peek at her pickup driving past. If only it were her own paranoia and imagination, but Cheryl knows they really are watching.

It's what a lot of them do to pass any given day, anyway. Her arrest has only heightened the drama on Turquoise Lane. She mutters under her breath at them. Like it or not, her arrest has only heightened the drama on Turquoise Lane.

She mutters under her breath at them. "Yeah, it's the murderer. Take a good look." Cheryl tries not to be annoyed with them. She would be curious, too.

It makes her want a drink. So, instead of going into her place, she walks the path to the Boney sisters' trailer. Say what you want about the warring sisters, at least they haven't cut her off yet, like nearly everyone else.

She knocks at their nicely kept up 40-foot Laredo. She hears what sounds like the Shopping Channel in the background.

Patty Boney opens the door, then draws back as though she smells something that stinks. She closes the door to only a crack. "Oh. Cheryl."

"Just wondered if your shopping list was ready." Cheryl normally does a couple of runs each week for them.

"I'll get it," Patty says curtly, moving to the kitchen counter. "But we're looking for somebody else after this."

Her sister Betty's voice comes from another room. "Who is it?"

"Nobody," Patty assures her.

Cheryl feels herself slump with disappointment. "Oh, no. Not you all, too." Then, suddenly feeling the need to defend herself, she adds, "You know, I didn't do it."

Patty swells up. "Oh, we know exactly what you've been doing. It's been going on for years."

Stunned, Cheryl shakes her head. "What's been going on for years?"

Betty shows up, standing at her sister's back. "Patty, stop it now." She gives an apologetic eye roll to Cheryl. "People are saying . . . oh, it's too stupid to even repeat."

Patty interrupts. "Where'd you get that eye patch,

anyway?"

"From Astrid down at the John Deere."

Patty nods. "I thought I'd seen it before." She studies Cheryl a moment, then says in a tone of pity, "You know it doesn't hide who you are, hon, don't you?"

Cheryl lets the dig pass, but asks again, "What's been going on for years?" The sisters exchange sharp looks, neither willing to get into it.

"Please. Tell me," Cheryl insists.

Betty sighs and glares at Patty. "Why did you even bring it up?" Then she turns to Cheryl. "Some people think you've been skimming money from them."

It feels like the last straw. "What? But you know that's not true."

"Of course, we do," Betty says. Another odd exchange of looks between the sisters. Cheryl senses something going on in Patty's pale, angular face that she can't quite read.

Patty Boney has always been something of a mystery to locals. While cleaning their mobile home, Cheryl has noticed studio pictures of her, back in her 20's probably, when she was softly seductive, a long mane of auburn hair caressing her shoulders, her youthful eyes brimming with dreams.

It has always been amazing to Cheryl, the transformation of that voluptuous face into the spiteful, brittle creature Patty has become.

Now that she thinks about it, Patty seemed to avoid Effie,

even though neither of them ever mentioned anything about it. Had something happened between the two of them?

"How long did you two know Effie?"

The sisters almost blush. Betty stares at her sister, who clams up.

"I'm sorry," Cheryl finally says. "I'm trying to find out everything I can about who could have murdered her. I just thought . . .."

Betty says, "We've always known her. We grew up together."

"Can you tell me anything about her and her husband, Ben?"

"That worthless dog?" Betty spits out.

Patty suddenly starts back to the T.V. "I'm going to miss out on the Daily Special. Their cashmere sweaters with the pearls are about to go on sale." She sits and turns up the volume. "I can't bid with you two talking. You need to go on, Cheryl."

Cheryl lowers her voice but keeps talking to Betty. "It's just Effie never told me about him."

Betty speaks low. "Never told nobody she didn't have to. She sure didn't shed any tears for that hound dog when he run off."

"He ran off with somebody else?" Cheryl asks.

"Nobody knows for sure. Just up and disappeared . . . over 30 years ago." Then Betty remembers something.

"You know, who you might talk to is Annie Faye, old colored gal that takes care of the cabin? Still works for Cliff and the witch. Go see her. She'll have some poop on Ben."

"I haven't heard that name in . . . she's still alive?"

"Too ornery to die," Betty says and opens the door for Cheryl.

"Thanks, Betty." As she nears her mobile home, it strikes her again how good it feels, knowing she didn't have sex with Doyle.

That does more to restore faith in herself, even if it was a fluke. In a week filled with cringes and shame, the universe has looked out for her, again. Whatever else, she can at least cross wanton hook-ups off her list of sins.

By the time she gets close to her place, Josey is hollering from the porch. "Cheryl. Noah's on the phone."

She hurries inside to the phone. "Hi, Noah."

"Can you come out, maybe? I found some interesting stuff on Ben and Cracker."

"No kidding? Me, too. I tried to call you earlier."

"My truck picked up a nail on the way home or I'd have come into town."

"Don't you have a spare?"

Noah chuckled. "About that . . . ."

"Okay, got it."

Then he laughs at himself. "I know, it's so cliched poor Indian. Sorry."

"I'm on my way." Cheryl feels lighter at the thought of seeing him. From somewhere the earthy smell of chrysanthemums makes her grin.

CHAPTER TWENTY-EIGHT

Noah's hound dogs bark and swarm around Cheryl's pickup as she pulls in front of his place. "Hi, dogs. Getting to know me, huh?" They allow her to pat their heads, a sure sign of acceptance.

Before she can knock, Noah opens the door, looking like he just stepped out of the shower. He's wrapped in a huge towel, his long hair loose and wet.

"You were quick. Sorry, just let me throw my clothes on." He leaves the door open for her and he heads back down the hall. "There's fresh coffee if you want some. And I like the eye patch," he hollers back to her.

Cheryl finds herself watching his disappearing back, still damp with water drops. Not a gym-sculpted set of muscles, but naturally built because of mountain climbing and working the land.

She feels a flush on her cheeks at the sight of him and immediately castigates herself. *Don't even think about it, kiddo.*

It's more reasonable to dismiss rather than entertain any possibilities, anyway. Other than occasional one-nighters with guys like Doyle, no man has really looked at since the accident. The scars, even the small ones on her face, don't seem to put guys off. But the second they see Cheryl on her feet, limping, it's written all over their faces. *Gimp.*

Noah is back in five minutes, during which time she has

poured herself some strong coffee and is looking out the kitchen window over his farm. Horses graze in a nearby field. Squeaks and grunts emanate from a chicken coop and pig pen closer to the house.

"Sorry to make you wait. I figured I'd be ready by the time you got here," he says.

"No problem. I just jumped in the truck and headed out." *Because I couldn't wait to see you.*

He grins at her. "Here's one for you. You know the top thing you'll never hear an Indian say?"

She smiles, uncertain of his joking tone. "No . . . ."

"I got four new tires and paid-up insurance. Let's go to the pow wow." Of the two of them, he laughs the loudest.

"I'll take you into town to get a new tire."

"Thanks." He points to her eyepatch. "Hey, you seeing double?"

Cheryl shrugs. "Maybe a little."

"Well, I like the satin patch, but that's nothing to mess around with." Off her silence, he leans down to stare directly into her eye. "Any headaches? The truth now."

"No, not since the first day." It is true. They've gone away."

"That's good. I won't bug you, but if the headaches come back, I'll haul you to the nearest doctor, even if it's kicking and screaming."

He spreads out some official looking documents on the small kitchen table. "Now. Take a look."

"What've you got?"

"The military record on Ben is pretty much what we already know. He suddenly goes AWOL in '56, and nobody knows why. Doesn't pick up his stuff at the base. Showed no signs of planning to leave town. Declared dead in '64.

"Right."

"The surprise, and I'm still not sure how I never knew this before, is that after Ben Lawrence married Effie, he and Cracker, Sr. apparently did put their heads together about the treasure."

Cheryl's mouth drops. "Wow. How did you . . .?"

"Gray Bear, one of our leaders, told me."

"The war hero?"

"Yeah. His father is still an elder, and his memory is going, unfortunately, but Gray Bear says his old man can remember Cracker's dad coming around a long time ago, with a young white guy with him. They showed him a map and fished around for leads."

"The original map? On leather?"

"No, it was drawn on a piece of paper, which may be why none of the elders took them seriously. But it could have been copied from the original rawhide one."

"Ben could have done that and Effie none the wiser.

When was this?"

"Gray Bear guessed the early fifties, maybe?"

"The time fits. You think Ben found Effie's map and got Cracker's father to help him with it."

"Cracker Sr. was a respected treasure hunter back in the day. Enjoyed regional fame for it. Where else do you think Cracker Jr. got all the material for his books?"

Another thought pops into Cheryl's head. "Ben is Cliff's uncle. Maybe Cliff knew about it. That would change everything.

"It's possible. Cliff is what? Mid-forties? He would have still been a kid when all this happened.

"Doesn't mean he didn't have big ears," Cheryl says.

Noah nods. "So, what did you find out?"

"After I left last night, I went by Cracker's store."

"By yourself? I told you . . . .."

"I know, but it was just a whim as I was driving by."

She puts up a hand. "Don't start. He was on the phone with somebody. I overheard him. It was a creepy conversation. About how he's taking the biggest risk, and he doesn't like where things are heading."

"He never said the name of who he talked to?"

"No, but he was mad, said they weren't holding up their end, and if they didn't, he'd dump the whole deal."

He shakes his head in thought. "Doesn't sound like good-old-boy Cracker talking."

"It sounds like he's right in the middle of this."

"It does." Noah's phone rings. "Hello." He squints his eyes. "Where?" He puts his hand over the receiver, "Can you give me a ride to Elk Mountain?" She nods.

"I'm on my way, Chief." Noah hangs up. "Hikers found someone a ravine in Elk Mountain. They need me."

She follows him as far as the hall. "Dead?"

"Don't know yet. But Chief says it looks like the body's wrapped in something. Not a good sign." He comes back with a huge duffle bag and mountain climbing gear.

Twenty minutes later, they pull up into a parking area with the best access to the site. Asa Bointy is there, waiting in the Medicine Wheel cruiser. The hikers, a trio of teenagers, sit nearby, visibly shaken.

"Sure glad you were home, Noah." Bointy acknowledges Cheryl with a nod. "Cheryl. It doesn't look good. Lucky for us these kids have good eyes." He hands Noah his binoculars. "Looks like a body to me. What do you think?"

Noah looks and nods. "Yeah, I think so, too."

"The wrapping blends into the rocks. It could've been there for days before anyone noticed it."

Noah assesses the situation as he gears up. "Looks like somebody just dropped it off the cliff there."

Cheryl looks over the edge and shudders. "That must be

at least a thirty-foot drop."

Noah buckled up his rappelling vest. "With some luck, the initial fall may not have been that far. Maybe it rolled down part of the way."

Bointy comes over with a two-way radio, their communication while Noah is below. They double-check the frequency.

Cheryl peers over the edge at the narrow ravine, which slices between the faces of the cliff in a deep gash. The body is caught between two stone formations, stopping its fall all the way to the bottom. Now it lies beside an unforgiving, vertical face, which Noah is preparing to descend.

The closer look makes Cheryl back away from the edge with a shiver. Cracker's words are so recent in her mind not to associate them. Could this be "dumping the whole business?"

She hurries over to Noah, who is about to go down. "Be careful. Good luck."

"Thanks," he says, "but listen, this will take quite a while—just for me to get down there. Go on. You don't want to see this."

Chief Bointy comes over to her. "Could you give me a hand, Cheryl? These poor kids . . . they're really shook up." He nods toward the three pale teenagers. "Shelby's on his way, but could you maybe give them a ride to their car? It's just a few miles back, where they hiked in from."

"Sure," she says, "whatever I can do."

"It's fine," Noah says. "The chief'll give me a ride."

"No, I'll be back for you. Take care."

"I always do." He goes to his entry point on the cliff. She sees him pause for a moment, eyes closed, as though saying a little prayer before he moves off into the canyon face to begin his descent.

Cheryl gathers up the teens and is pulling out when Chief Bointy's mobile cruiser phone rings. He waves them down. She stops the pickup alongside him.

"Good news. Silas has regained consciousness," he says.

CHAPTER TWENTY-NINE

Cheryl feels something wound tight inside her break up. She ignores all the Wildlife Refuge speed limits driving back to the parking lot that accesses Elk Mountain. When she drops the boys at their car, they murmur their thanks.

Floor boarding the truck to Southwest Memorial Hospital, she steps into the lobby less than a half hour later. The first person she finds on Silas's floor is the night nurse.

"Silas is conscious?" Cheryl asks.

"About an hour ago," the nurse says.

"Has he said anything?"

The nurse laughs. "Are you kidding? It's like he's making up for lost time."

"Thanks," Cheryl waves back to her. She takes off her eyepatch—no need to freak him out—then taps on Silas's door before slipping inside. "Silas, it's Cheryl."

Before she sees him, she hears him snapping out orders. "Get this vampire off me." Hovering over Silas, a harried technician tries to draw a blood sample.

"Just hold still—one more second." the technician pleads.

"I hate needles. Get him away," Silas says.

The techie's tired eyes look to Cheryl for possible help.

"Silas, they have to do this. I'm sure it's for some good reason.

The techie-vampire raises his hands in good natured defeat. "Tell you what, I'll come back around later."

"Ha!" Silas harrumphs at his victory, then motions Cheryl over.

She pulls up a chair and takes his hand. "You seem awful feisty for somebody that just came out from under."

Silas's hands are trembling, despite his bravado. "I've been out almost two days, they tell me. What did I miss? Tell me everything."

"First, everyone wants to know who did this to you."

"I didn't see 'em. I was going somewhere—oh, no, it was the damn dogs. I was trying to feed them, and they start yelping all of a sudden, at something behind me. Next thing I know, somebody's beating me up."

"You could be dead, Silas," she says with sympathy, squeezing his hand.

"They can't kill me," he announces, jutting his chin out in Spartacus-like defiance. For a moment Cheryl glimpses the young man who gutted it out in the death camps, who beat the odds, too proud to give in.

"Now tell me what you and my niece have found out?"

She gives him a rundown of what's been happening, then

asks, "I know you weren't around when Effie originally got that map, but did she ever say anything about anybody else seeing it? Like early on, maybe? When she was still married?"

Silas wrinkles his nose in disgust. "You're saying the husband?"

"Maybe Ben, yes. Or somebody he knew? Maybe Old Cracker? Or even Cliff?"

"Effie never said anything like that. But from what she told me, none of them would've passed up the chance."

"What about Ben's brother? Cliff's father. Was he around?"

"She never mentioned him. But he's dead, I think."

"I just don't get how, after almost fifty years, suddenly it pops us again. Somebody didn't want me to track down what happened to the prospector's nephew--the one who attacked the doctor who treated Charlie Edgars when he was dying. They destroyed the microfiche that showed his picture. Maybe he came back into the picture?"

Cheryl looks at Silas's drawn face and realizes she's pushing things. "I'm sorry. Here I am, buzzing along, and what you need is rest. I'll leave so you can."

"No, I think you may . . . what if Goob Edgars died and what he knew came out." Silas studies the ceiling tiles with squinted eyes, as though the answer lingered up there. Then his eyes pop open. "You know who could help? Josey. She did all my Auschwitz research, tracing family and friends. She'd send it to me from wherever she was working.

"That's perfect, Silas."

A uniform comes bearing a lunch platter.

"About time," Silas says. "I'm hungry enough to eat a bear."

"I'll leave you to it. Be back as soon as I can."

By the time she climbs in her red pickup, she feels a little dizzy from seeing her surroundings in double. She pulls the patch on and gets her bearings by slowing down enough to consider the next right thing to do.

Cliff and Katie's cabin is on the way back to Medicine Wheel, and she still needs to talk about the codicil to Effie's will. And maybe run into Annie Faye Johnson, who could have some answers.

CHAPTER THIRTY

Artillery tests boom as Cheryl hurries the red pickup down the road. Winter alfalfa flaps alongside the shoulders. As she turns into the cypress tree-lined drive to the cabin, it looks like a full-scale construction site.

A huge yellow backhoe grinds away in the back yard, making an enormous hole, while construction company vehicles and workers swarm the grounds. Cheryl grins to see Katie shaking a scolding finger in the face of the backhoe operator. *Of course,* Cheryl thinks, *she will insinuate herself into every last detail.*

As Cheryl pulls up to the house, she sees Cliff sneaking a cigarette out on the front steps. He looks happy to be hiding out from Katie, the wife who "reformed" his tobacco habit, or so she thinks.

Cliff looks up, guilty for a second, then seeing it's Cheryl, relaxes and takes a last deep drag. "Well. Cheryl."

"Hi, Cliff." She climbs down from the truck.

"What brings you out here?"

"Though I'd check out the new pool."

"How'd you know about that?"

"Saw Astrid when I went by John Deere to hunt you

down. Wasn't much going on, so we visited a little."

Cliff puts his butt in his pocket. Cheryl notices he doesn't toss it, even here in the country, but she's pretty sure it's so he won't get caught, not ecological concerns.

The machinery from the back grows louder, so she forces herself to talk up. "How big a pool you digging?"

"I'd show you, but it's only hard-hats today."

Cheryl grins. "And Katie, of course. I saw her supervising as I drove up." He colors a little. "So, Cliff, I'm really here about some lost codicil. What's going on?"

Suddenly, he's preoccupied with his manicured nails. "I'm not going to talk about the details."

"You know what I think?" Cheryl watches him closely as she braves her subject. "The inventory of Effie's estate will show you don't really own this place."

He fixes her with a hard stare. "What?"

"Effie as much as told me you two never made payments to her, to speak of."

He flashes with anger, then looks away.

So it is true, Cheryl thinks. Their mortgage went the way of so many family debts, never paid in full, because Cliff bet his aunt would never take him to court. They probably stiffed her for the entire amount.

"You don't know what you're talking about," Cliff insists. "I think it's time for you to leave."

"Fine I'm free all next week, whenever you want to get together with the lawyers."

Katie comes around the corner, looking suspicious. She raises her eyebrows at them. Cheryl senses--woman's intuition—with some astonishment, that Katie is ticked because she doesn't want her husband alone with another woman. *As though I would have designs on Cliff.*

Katie's voice is ice. "What's going on?"

"Just letting Cliff know when I'm free to read the codicil," Cheryl assures her.

"Our lawyer will handle that," Katie shoots back.

Cheryl hurries back toward her pickup. "Oh, by the way, does Annie Faye, I think her name is . . . does she still work for you all?"

Katie looks disgusted. "If you can call what she does work. I haven't been able to find her all morning long."

"I told you I sent her into town to pick up some things." Cliff's irritation is just under his skin.

Katie's lips push out as she scoffs. "Like she should be driving at her age."

CHAPTER THIRTY-ONE

When the woman regains consciousness, her breathing is so ragged, it frightens her. And each intake brings wracking pain from her rib cage and lower back. Her hands are tied in front. Nothing else is bound, but her entire body is wrapped in something. A blanket? A rug?

She has no idea where she is, but it's outside, and it is freezing. Her bare feet feel disconnected from the rest of her. When she tries to wiggle her toes, there is only numbness. A strong draft of wind seems to come from below her, seeping into the crevices of her wrapping. When she opens her eyes, she can only see bits of sunshine poking through the weave of her shroud.

How did she get here? Her mind is blank. She tries to move her hands and torso, but the more she struggles the more the pain swallows her up.

Then she thinks there's a voice. Or maybe it's an auditoy hallucination. She becomes very still. Words echo from above her.

"Hey, Chief, I see movement. Call for help."

'In spite of her agony, she tries to rock her body, to assure them she is, yes, here and alive. She can't speak. Her voice is submerged in her sand-dry throat.

She hears the voice again, speaking loudly through

whistles of wind. "Hey, we see you. It's okay. You don't need to struggle. We're on our way. We got you."

It is the first moment of relief in, what? Three? Four days? *Somebody's got her.* It is nothing short of a miracle. But her nostrils are badly stopped up. She's afraid if she lets herself cry, she won't be able to breathe.

****

Noah detects more movement in the canvas wrapping before he gets down to it. By the time he reaches the victim and feverishly cuts through one end of the rolled canvas, the movement has stopped. He finds a faint pulse under a full head of hair, then see it's a woman. That gives him a jolt.

Thank the Spirits this will be a rescue, not a recovery.

After he uncovers her battered face, he's amazed she's not dead from shock or exposure. She's been down in the canyon all night, it looks like, and what he can glimpse of her body under the canvas is bruised and swollen. In his many years of rescue work, he has only seen one other person fall this far down in a rocky canyon. And that man died before they could get to him.

As he prepares her for transport, the wop-wop-wop of the Medivac copter can be heard coming in. That was quick, he thinks gratefully. Way to go, Chief.

Noah situates himself far enough out from the cliff wall that the chopper can hover directly above them and drop a rescue board straight down to him. It dangles from the copter as he lashes her onto the board, an arduous task given their position. The wind whips through the small outcropping of rock where they are precariously balanced.

His legs throb and threaten to cramp as he struggles to keep them both steady enough to finish the job. He wishes now that he had requested a medic with the board, but that could be even more dangerous. Noah knows he can do it, even though his energy ebbs by the minute.

When his fingers cramp up on him, he stops and shuts his eyes for a moment to gather strength. Noah thinks on the ghosts of his ancestors all around in these mountains. He asks for the strength to save this woman. He imagines breathing in their powerful spirit as he calls on every last bit of stamina to help her along.

Finally, he has her secured. On his signal, the pilot slowly pulls her up to safety. The medic awaits her in the copter and will start treatment the moment they pull her aboard.

As the Medivac sweeps her away, the canyon falls silent again, save the hum of the wind. Noah sits for a moment, willing his hands and legs not to seize up. As his body revives, his sigh of relief is slowly replaced by a sense of rage. The brutality of it nauseates him.

He takes his time climbing back to the surface, too exhausted to do anything but ascend slowly and steadily. When he arrives at the top of the canyon, Chief Bointy is waiting. Assistant Chief Myers is on scene and stands talking over the cruiser phone.

"Amazing work, Noah," Bointy says, offering him a hand. "Don't know how you got her out of that wedge. I thought she was a goner for sure. "

Noah shrugs off his heavy pack and sinks to the ground. With shaky hands, he gratefully accepts some coffee from Bointy's thermos. After he catches his breath, he asks, "What is going on, Chief?"

"We'll have to find out who she is first, then . . .."

"No, I mean here. What the hell is happening in Medicine Wheel? Miss Lawrence tortured to death, Cheryl attacked, Silas beaten up? Now this?"

Shifting his cigar stub from one hand to the other, Bointy nods. "It's got to be a record of some kind."

"Whoever threw her down that canyon never expected she'd live to tell the tale."

"Yeah, well, thanks to you, maybe they'll get a nasty surprise, huh?"

Shelby hangs up the cruiser's phone and heads toward them. "Southwest Memorial has her in I.C.U."

"What else did they say?" Noah asks.

"They don't know anything yet. They'll keep us posted." He looks at Noah. "That was an incredible thing you just did, Noah. Did you know who she was?"

"Never saw her before."

Bointy clicks his ballpoint, ready to write in his notepad. "How old, do you think?"

"Maybe forties, petite, no tats I could see, but I left her in the canvas wrap so she wouldn't freeze. It was a paint drop cloth, from the look of it. Reddish brown hair, in pretty good shape generally, it looked like. But filthy, scraped and bruised. Face so swollen I don't know if anybody will be able to recognize her."

Noah looks up to see Cheryl's red pickup swing into the parking lot. He loves that she came back for him. Right now it means everything.

She jumps out and hurries to him. "How did it go?"

Noah nods a tired smile and lifts himself off the ground. "We got her. And she's alive."

"Thank goodness. You look like you've been through hell."

He manages a tired grin. "But it had a good ending. Or, so far, anyway."

Shelby asks Bointy, "Should I head over to Southwestern, Chief? Check on her status?"

"Yeah, after she comes around, maybe she can tell us who did this," Bointy says.

"On it." Shelby jumps into the cruiser and takes off.

Bointy looks at Noah and Cheryl a moment, then says, "You two go on. I'll finish up here. Send me the bill, Noah."

"I'll do that." Noah's bones creak as he gets up and stretches. "Ever think maybe this isn't your month to retire, Asa?" The sheriff gives a tired nod of his head.

Noah loads his gear into the back of Cheryl's pickup. "Anything new on who attacked Silas, Chief?"

"No, but there is good news for you, Cheryl. We can rule you out." Bointy nods toward Noah. "Your Pawnee buddy there alibied you for the time Silas was attacked."

Noah tells Cheryl, "We also talked about the fact that whoever beat up Silas is likely the same one who killed Effie."

Bointy smiles at Noah, seeing where he's going with this. "Okay, don't push it now." But he turns to Cheryl. "Nobody's officially apologizing yet, but Buddy Mason may have jumped the gun, having us arrest you."

"The same goes for your Assistant Chief," Noah says, "who wants to impress everybody as he makes his move to take over your job when you retire."

"Shelby is trying to score points, granted. Doesn't mean he got it all wrong."

Noah is reminded of how decent the Chief is. Basically, a humble man, one of the few around in power who doesn't take himself too seriously. In a hurry to retire, Bointy was probably not at his best when his Assistant, who seems unfamiliar with humility, started chomping at the big for a bigger title.

The problem is that Shelby Myers doesn't have enough experience to bide his time, gather all the evidence, then put the whole picture together. He impresses Noah as a hot shot with good looks and charm, bright enough, but with ambition his overriding motivator.

This time, though, the Assistant Chief wasn't just overzealous with parking or speeding tickets. This time it was a murder charge, and Cheryl was the one who got jammed up. Noah isn't sure why that upsets him so much, but he wonders what it means for future law enforcement in Medicine Wheel.

When Noah and Cheryl drive away from Elk Mountain, he finally begins to relax. His tight muscles let go, and a sense of exhaustion comes on so strong, his eyelids go heavy. His shoulders still throb, and his neck feels clamped tight.

He feels Cheryl's hand touch his. "It's getting near dark. Do you want to just go home?" Or what?"

"I want some scrambled eggs with cheese on top," he says.

"Alright. Coming right up."

He slumps back in the front seat and stretches his long legs. As his head turns toward her, she is framed against a peach sun just starting to set. There's something about her face, with no makeup, the way the breeze blows her hair back, the curve of her nose, even her eyepatch . . . that touch him.

He can still remember the school gym bleachers, watching her play basketball, her quickness and strong hands, and, of course, her deadly aim around the key. She was the local star, too high up for him to even think of flirting with. He sees how she's been humbled by the twists in her life, can feel the undercurrent of sadness that is part of her now. He imagines it's because she can't forgive herself. Yet it makes her natural beauty more complete. Like soldiers who have looked inside death and return to the world with different eyes.

Noah feels safe with her, even though there's no logic to it. He folds his torso across the seat and lays his head on her leg. He feels her tighten at first and then relax. After a moment, her hand strokes his long hair.

Noah realizes he's silently crying. He doesn't want her to see. He isn't even sure where it is coming from, but he can't make himself stop.

CHAPTER THIRTY-TWO

Cheryl feels the involuntary tremors in Noah's neck. She can't take him to a restaurant in this shape, and she doesn't want to take him to her place, where Josey and the four Chihuahuas are still camped out. So, she heads to his farm. On the way she picks up bacon and eggs at an I-44 quick stop. By the time she climbs back in the truck, Noah has fallen asleep.

His kitchen is clean and neat, whether it's because he keeps it that way or rarely uses it, she can't tell. Soon the smell of bacon fills the room. Noah lets her cook while he sits at the table and drinks fresh coffee. Cheryl's culinary skills generally suck, but she can scramble eggs without burning them.

Noah seems to agree as he scarves everything down.

"You want some more?" She nudges her plate toward him. "I'm not hungry."

"That's plenty for now. Delicious." His neck cracks as he moves it. "Now if I can get this ache out of my shoulders . . . man, I feel like I got stretched on a medieval rack."

"How did you do it?"

"I let myself get tense while I was down there. I know better, but it still happens."

Cheryl puts both their plates on the counter and walks behind him. Before she touches his shoulders, she asks, "Want me to . . . ?"

He sighs. "I'll take anything."

His muscles are tight as she works her fingers into his shoulder blades. After a few minutes, his head drops back toward her. They've never been quite this close, and there's no mistaking the energy between them. It seems to fill the small kitchen, even stronger because neither of them is sure how to acknowledge it.

Finally, feeling the heat in her body too much to bear, she takes her hands away and steps back. This is what she swore not to do any more. "I'd better quit," she says simply.

He doesn't say anything. He doesn't need to. She can feel him wanting her. But he only watches her as she looks self-consciously at him.

"Well," she says, picking up her purse and standing by the table. "I'm going to go now."

He looks up at her, his eyes unreadable. "It's my ex-wife. You know."

"Your wife? What do you mean?" Then Cheryl realizes. "Oh, of course, she was an addict, too. So, you know . . . how this needs to go."

"I swore I'd never get involved with anyone like that again. I'm sorry, I didn't mean--"

Cheryl reddens. Of course, he doesn't want her, she realizes. How could she have misread things so badly? "No, I understand. I get it."

"You do? Because I don't." His eyes are hollow lights as he glances over at the picture of the Native woman in the marriage picture. "Never did. With her, it was like living with shadows. Ghosts. Someone who was never quite there. I can't do that again." He stares down at the table, his face twisted and tight. "Even though I really . . . really like you. Always have."

Now the energy between them has shifted but is no less intense. Cheryl sits back down and studies his long, angular face.

"I wish I could tell you why I drank . . . drink . . . to the point of destruction. If only there was some dark family secret to blame it on, some trauma. But the truth is, I was loved as a child, even cherished, I believe. I was given everything, a good home, education, honors. I was one of the lucky ones. So . . . I have no excuse, no reason."

Her breathing is ragged now. She has never said any of this out loud before, not even in meetings. "And I don't blame my parents for disowning me. I was their golden child and I turned around and broke their hearts. It's what I deserve."

He starts to say something, but she puts a hand up to stop him. She must finish.

"There's something not right with me, I'm afraid. I have this—like a deep ache and it won't go away. Like a hole I keep trying to fill, but I can't." A dry chuckle escapes her. "I haven't had a drink for three days now, and before I went out this last time, I had chalked up two years of sobriety. But I can't tell you why I picked up that drink. I want to be sober, more than anything. And I really don't plan to drink again. I don't want to. Yet I know what I am. And I can't promise you that I won't."

He takes her hand. Something in his touch runs through

her in the kindest way, like when someone strikes a match in the dark. Outside an owl hoots, and dogs howl.

Cheryl feels the scruff of his stubble when he kisses her. She smells the natural sweetness of his body even through his salty skin. She wants to get lost in him, in his endless arms and body. But she doesn't dare.

"You're emotionally exhausted," she says, gently pushing him away. "We both are."

"No, it's okay," he says.

"No, I'm afraid to ruin it." She touches his face. "You're special. You understand?"

"Ssssh," he whispers in her ear and removes her eye patch. Noah puts his long arms under her t-shirt and pulls her in to him, and finally Cheryl lets herself go. Lost inside the pounding of her heart, she wraps herself around him. It feels almost unbearably beautiful.

CHAPTER THIRTY-THREE

The next morning, after a long, hot shower, Cheryl, in her favorite chenille robe, nests in her recliner. She forced herself to drive home from Noah's late last night. When she pulled in, the Crime Scene ribbon around Silas's place was gone, and both the dogs and Josey had moved back there.

No more Grand Central Station. The stillness during her first cup of coffee makes her close her eyes. She noticed when she awoke earlier, that her double vision seems almost back to normal. Her thoughts turn to Noah and last night.

When her phone rings, she hurries to pick it up, thinking it might be him. Instead, Silas's voice booms through the line.

"Come and get me. Now."

"Silas? They're releasing you?" This doesn't sound right. It's too soon, given the shape he was in yesterday.

There is a long pause. "Just come and get me."

"I'll be happy to, but I want to talk to the doctor--"

The click of the phone disconnecting annoys her. That's all she needs, Silas going all dramatic on her. She looks around for the note with his room number.

The phone rings again. *Wow, that was quick.* It usually takes him longer to come to his senses when he pulls one of his melodramatic moves.

"What is going on, Silas?" she answers.

From the other end, her dad's voice sounds a little shaky. "Cheryl?" It sounds like traffic in the background.

"Daddy? Is that you?"

His voice is hoarse with emotion, but he pulls himself together with a cough. "How's my little girl?"

"Oh, I'm muddling through . . . you know. How did you find out?"

"We still have plenty of friends back there who can't wait to pass on bad news." Cheryl shakes her head. Of course.

"It's so awful what happened to poor Effie," he says. "I was afraid you might be in jail."

"Silas bailed me out."

"How is Silas?"

So, he doesn't know that part. "He's in the hospital. In fact, he was just calling to tell me to come get him." She doesn't really want to get into it, but does anyway. After all, her father loves Silas. They had years of morning coffee together. She hears her father whoosh out air at the end of the story.

"Poor guy. We hadn't heard that yet."

After a moment, Cheryl asks, "Where are you? Is that cars going by?"

"A campground in Delaware. I'm calling from a phone in

their office. It's right beside a highway."

Cheryl knows he sneaked out to the R.V. park office to call her. If her mother knew what he was doing, she would forbid it.

"I appreciate that you called, Dad. I know it wasn't easy."

His voice breaks. "I love you, kiddo . . . we both do."

The difference being that you don't pass judgment. "I love you, too, Dad."

He insists on hearing all the details of her arrest and how Bointy has been treating her. Cheryl shares her suspicions, her questions . . . all except Doyle, anyway. Her father seems hungry to hear even the minutiae. Things only a parent could listen to so intently.

Cheryl asks, "You lived close to Effie a long time here in the park. Do you remember anything about her and Ben?"

"She was widowed by the time we moved in there. Ella Mae did a lot of church work with her, but . . . ." He pauses.

Cheryl waits.

He says, "You know, there was something. It may not be anything, but are the Boney sisters still there?"

"Yeah, crazy as ever."

"Well, I don't know what it's worth, but you mother told me once that they knew a lot more about Effie and Ben's marriage than they let on."

"Did she say how she knew?"

"Woman's intuition was all she said."

"That could be a huge help."

"I'll see if I can finagle anything more out of her that might help. Look, we'll be here for a couple of weeks. I'm going to give you this number in case you need money . . . or anything. I mean it, now. They'll come get me from the office here."

Cheryl writes it down, knowing she'll never dial it. But if it helps her father. Lost in a loveless marriage, he doesn't know anything else. Watching his once powerful, athletic body grow stooped and his face sag too soon, had been hard.

Bud Jackson was the one who first showed her a basketball, how to shoot with the right arc and follow through. To understand the shot is not over and done because it leaves your hands. And she had never once felt as if he wished he had a son. In a loud, sweaty gym, game on the line, it was always his voice, low out of the bleachers, that cut through the crowd, like he was right by her side.

At some point Cheryl finally realized her father was too gentle for beautiful, spiteful Ella Mae. She had dominated both of them through manipulation and shame. Cheryl had long thought that her father had anger buried so deep he didn't know he had it any more.

"I'll call if I need anything. You're too good." They talk a few minutes more, carefully avoiding anything about her mother, before hanging up.

Cheryl refills her coffee and stands looking out the kitchen window at the trees behind her mobile home. She'd like to hang out here longer, but Silas's call makes her get moving. In jeans and sweatshirt, Cheryl heads toward the Boney's before she gets in her pickup.

No soon is she within earshot than she hears bickering voices. The moment she knocks, Betty peers through the front window.

"Who is that?" Patty asks.

"It's Cheryl."

"I don't want to talk to her."

Cheryl's interest is piqued now. She stands in the door frame. "What's going on?"

Patty shrinks back as if avoiding grease from a frying pan. But Betty takes her firmly by the arm. "Come in, Cheryl. I thought you'd be back over."

Cheryl senses something big is happening, but they look like they don't know what to do next. "Should we sit down?"

As they settle around the sisters' living room, Betty keeps an eagle eye on her sister, who no longer looks as though she's ready to bolt, but is not yet comfortable either.

Cheryl tries to break the ice. "Is this a bad time, ladies?"

"No, no, it's fine," Betty insists, with a glance at her sister, who is rubbing her hands like she's applying hand cream.

"The fact is," Cheryl begins, "I have a feeling that you two know more about what's going on than you indicated yesterday. Have either of you got something to tell me? Because I think you know that there's more happening her than a robbery.

I know you know—everyone's talking about it—that it was a treasure map to a cache of Mexican coins that got Effie killed."

The sisters exchange glances but neither speaks.

"Look," Cheryl says kindly, "I'm not pointing any fingers here. Just, please, what do you know?"

Betty nudges Patty, who gives a big sigh before saying, "I may know something about . . . Effie's murder . . . maybe." Her tone is halting and tentative.

Cheryl's pulse quickens. "Anything could help."

Betty Boney's knees bounce with impatience. "Just tell her, for god's sake."

Cheryl put up a hand, trying to tell Betty to cool it. Then she waits for Patty. "In your own time, Patty. No hurry. What do you know?"

"It was years ago. I made a mistake." She stops, as if she might break down if she continues. But she somehow does. "I had an affair with Ben Lawrence."

Cheryl struggles to hide her astonishment. She's afraid any reaction could spook Patty into silence. "I see," she says simply.

"I know it was wrong."

Cheryl keeps her tone casual. "Lots of people have affairs, Patty."

Patty looks at Cheryl directly for the first time, her eyes dark with hurt. "I've paid the price for it, too. I know that now."

"You won't get any judgment from me, I can promise you that," Cheryl tells her. "But how does this relate to what happened to Effie."

Patty licks her lips then reaches into a jar on a side table. "Because I know that Ben is somewhere on an island, if he's still alive, of course. Living off his stolen fortune."

She retrieves a perfectly polished coin, so old its intricate carvings and Spanish engravings speak of another century.

Cheryl's hand shakes as she reaches for it. "Ben gave you this?"

Betty can hold back no longer. "Yes. Right after he gave her his promise of undying love and running off together."

Patty flashes an angry look at her sister, then lets it go. "I got took."

Cheryl tries to pull the threads of the story together. "But you and Ben?"

"I was a kid, and he was a dashing soldier. I was smitten."

"Ben told her Effie had gotten all eat up with Jesus," Betty throws in.

"That's just how he put it," Patty confirms. *Eat up with Jesus.*"

"He told Patty that Effie henpecked him night and day about getting saved, said he couldn't stand it anymore."

Patty nods. "It's a miracle I didn't get pregnant. I sure

didn't know much better."

"So, you were going to run off with him?" Cheryl asks.

"Oh yes," Patty says. "He it all planned out."

Cheryl's mentally tries to construct a timeline. "But he was still married to Effie. What about that?"

"He told me where we were headed, we wouldn't need to worry about marriage certificates. Or money. I wasn't so sure about that part, but he said it was all arranged, a place where we could live together forever on what he had."

Patty points to the coin. "He gave me that to prove it. Said there was plenty more where that came from."

"So, what happened?"

"He was supposed to pick me up at noon on the day we were leaving. He said no more than two suitcases, that we'd buy everything else on the drive to Galveston. We were supposed to leave on a boat from there."

Patty's eyes flash with life as the past comes close again. "I'd never been so excited. It was so romantic. I was so nuts about him, I really didn't even think about not seeing my sister, my family again. I thought my great life adventure was just beginning."

A stillness grabs the room. Then, after a few moments, Cheryl says," But he never showed up?"

Patty's face reverts to a lifeless, damaged visage. "Went without me. Never saw him again."

"Maybe it was something he couldn't help," Cheryl suggests. "An accident?"

Betty picks up the argument. "Then why did he just disappear off the face of the earth. Even if the worst happened, why wasn't his body ever discovered? And his fortune of old coins? All gone."

"And his car?" Cheryl asks.

"They found it at their cabin," Patty says.

"Where was Effie during all this?"

"He made sure she was staying with her parents that weekend," Patty explains. "She'd been doing that more and more, anyway, 'cause they were always fighting."

"Effie sold the car soon after. She didn't want anything to remind her of Ben," Betty says.

Longing fills Patty's face. "He always said he wanted to be the one who got away. I didn't even know what he meant. But that's what happened."

"It sounds like he loved you, Patty," Cheryl says. "Why would he ask you to run away with him if he didn't mean it?"

Betty hisses. "Because he was a mean, worthless piece of crap."

Cheryl shakes her head. "He wouldn't have given her one of the coins if that was the case. Why give away the fact that he had that kind of fortune? Do you have any idea what that's worth today?"

Patty shrugs. "I never checked, you know? Never had the heart to."

Cheryl wants to ask to take the coin with her but decides it's not going anywhere. She knows where it will be.

After she leaves the sisters, Cheryl climbs into her pickup. As a just-in-case afterthought, she opens the glove box and feels inside. Her dad's .22 is still there.

CHAPTER THIRTY-FOUR

Noah hurries out to meet Cheryl as she appears from her pickup. He kisses her with the giddiness of a teenager. He wants her all over again, even though he's still not sure exactly how it happened last night. One minute he was telling her why they couldn't get involved, and the next he wanted her so badly he could barely breathe.

"Sorry to attack you," he grins.

"Are you kidding? I love it."

He pulls her closer, kissing her again, wanting to take her inside. She would like it, too, he can tell.

"Not that I don't want to, I do. But . . . ." Cheryl says.

"Uh oh."

She sighs. "Silas called and said come get him. I think he's stirred up some trouble."

"First things first then," Noah concedes. "I want to see our mystery woman, too."

"Yeah. And we can pick up your tire on the way there."

"Sounds like a plan," he says.

As soon as they're on the road, Cheryl jumps into it. "I've got a big development. You won't believe who I talked to thirty minutes ago.

Noah hangs on to her every word as he hears Patty's story. It's almost enough to make him forget his aching body. Grinning ear to ear, he says, "So the elders were right. Ben Lawrence did find the James booty. Those old guys'll get a kick out of being right on that deal."

"Patty and Betty promised me they would tell Chief Bointy about everything this morning."

"So, Ben and Effie were living at the cabin then, but he had the treasure stowed away somewhere, to pick up before he flies the coop with his lover."

"Maybe even hidden at the cabin. They said Effie wasn't there that day but at her parents in Lawton, on account of everything going south in the marriage.

"Still . . .," Noah says, "Effie was smart. How could she not have known something was up? But, you know, maybe she did, on some level. He's not paying attention to her, he's feeling henpecked. She knew things weren't right."

"But did she know he's gotten to her prospector's map and found the treasure?" Cheryl asks.

"If he found the original map, drew a copy, then put it back . . . I can buy she didn't know. What I don't buy is Ben locating the treasure without any help. He wasn't a native of the area, not even a treasure hunter. He had to have help."

"Poor Patty," Cheryl says. "Betty was the only one she could confide in. Then Effie moves into the same mobile home park, and they end up neighbors. I wonder if Patty thought it was part of her penance."

They hit town and pull into *Eddy's New & Used Tires.*

Noah's lingering soreness from yesterday is almost forgotten as he throws the used tire into the back of Cheryl's pickup. Eddy knows better than to try to sell him a new one. Noah's good mood is such that he would like to spring for something better than a retread, but a look at his checkbook reminds him it's going to be another tight month. *Aren't they all?*

When he climbs back in the pickup, Cheryl's humming in the driver's seat. It's a cool fall day, the breeze pushing milky clouds across the sky at a clip. On the way out of Medicine Wheel, Cheryl tips her head toward the bank parking lot. "Looks like Cliff's car."

"Yeah. Why?"

"After we get Silas, I want to go out to the cabin again today, try to locate Annie Faye."

"The old woman who works for them?"

"Yeah. And it'd be better if Cliff and Katie weren't there." She shoots him a conspiratorial look, as if to say, *Are you with me?*

Noah grins. "Soon as we finish at the hospital."

A small contingent of reporters clusters around the entrance of SW Medical. He hasn't seen the morning paper, but Noah's radar tells him the rescue story has hit the airwaves. Every local plains paper worth its salt, and both state dailies, want the gruesome details.

"Let's go in through one of the side doors," he suggests. "Avoid these reporters." He doesn't really think he would be recognized, but doesn't want to deal with questions, just in case.

They slip in undetected and make their way to Silas's floor. When they walk into Room 203, he is still in his hospital gown, but up and packing his stuff in hospital plastic bags. But the real stunner is who is helping: Doyle Lowe.

Cheryl moves into alarm mode. "Silas, what are you doing?" Then to Doyle, "And what are you . . .?"

"He's helping me escape this insane asylum," Silas snaps. "You're late, Cheryl. I had to take charge myself." As he whirls around to her, he loses his balance. Doyle hurries over to steady him.

"I was just here for my nose," Doyle explains, his voice sounding like the foghorn rooster from ancient cartoons. He gives Cheryl a slitted glare through his swollen black and blue eyes. "I thought I'd drop by and see Silas since I was here."

"You got the doctor's okay for this, Silas?" Noah asks Silas.

"Don't need anybody's okay. I'm a hundred percent." Silas's voice is much stronger than his body is, though. He's unsteady on his feet.

"Sit down, Silas. You're dizzy, aren't you?" Cheryl asks.

"No, now, it's these damn cataracts, affecting my balance. And they strapped me down to the damn bed like a prisoner on the rack." No one in the room is about to respond to that.

"I get that," Cheryl says, "but Dr. Hokeah didn't call me to come get you, and he's the one who discharges you."

Noah quickly says, "Why don't I go find the doctor?" Noah offers and hurries out the door over Silas's protests.

It's a little awkward between Doyle and Cheryl. After a moment, she asks, "How's your nose?"

"Still hurts like a bitch. But the doctor made some adjustments today that he says will help."

"Good." She nods. "Good."

Silas gives an exasperated sigh. "For crying out loud, am I going to have to walk out of here on my own?"

CHAPTER THIRTY-FIVE

In the hall, Noah heads toward the nurse's station to try to find someone to page Dr. Hokeah. He sees Assistant Chief Shelby Myers, in jeans and boots, walking toward the room next door.

Noah nods to him. He met Myers when he was initially hired late last winter, but they rarely crossed paths until yesterday during the rescue.

"Glad to see you looking none the worse for wear," Shelby says.

"Not bad," Noah says. "You off duty?"

Myers shakes his head and gestures toward Room 201. "Hardly. Just got back from a shower to pull another shift guarding our Jane Doe."

Alright if I look in on her?" Noah asks.

"Be my guest, but I'm pretty sure she's in La-La Land."

Noah gingerly opens the door to the darkened room. The window blinds are closed and the usually bright blue-white lights that surround patients have been dimmed to a soft glow, more conducive to rest.

He stands at the end of the bed for a few moments and looks at the petite, red headed woman, buried alive in white bandages and blankets. Her breathing is slow, but steady. Bags of antibiotics, painkillers, and saline drip into her line.

"Sure glad you made it, Miss," Noah whispers. "You are a helluva fighter to come through this." He reaches for her free hand and holds it gently. Closing his eyes, he silently prays to his spirits to heal her and watch over her.

In a late reaction to being touched, the woman squeezes his hand. Noah recognizes that it's probably an automatic physical response to his holding her hand, but he wants to believe that something passed between them as he prayed. As though in answer, her eyes flutter open for a moment. Close. Then open again.

Noah looks around to see if a nurse or doctor might be around, but there's no one. He doesn't want to let go of her hand. Whatever it provoked, he wants to open her up more. Leaning closer into her, he says, "Can you hear me, ma'am?"

Her eyes blink, then remain half-open. Her mouth, chapped and swollen, parts a bit, but no sound comes out. Finally, Noah realizes he can hit the Call button on the side of her bed without releasing her hand and does. "I've called someone, okay?" he whispers to her.

A nurse is there within moments, followed quickly by Shelby Myers. "Is she conscious?" he asks.

"Opened her eyes," Noah says, keeping hold of the woman's hand but staying out of the nurse's way. "You're in the hospital," she enunciates carefully to the woman. "You've been in a bad fall, but you're doing great."

The woman squeezes Noah's hand in response. "I think

she hears you," he says and leans closer to the woman. "Can you tell us your name?"

The nurse offers her some water through a straw. "Probably too dry to talk, even if she's aware of us," she whispers to Noah. Then, in full voice to her patient, "You're safe now. You're in a hospital. You're going to be okay."

The woman takes a few sips of water, then, as quickly as she became conscious, she drafts back off. Noah and the nurse stand at the end of the bed, looking at her.

Shelby heads for the door. "I'll call the Chief. He'll want to know."

As she holds the straw so the woman can sip, she looks at crude, tattoo-like numbers on top of the patient's shoulder. "Did you notice that marking? Isn't that odd?" she asks Noah. "It's not professionally done."

"I missed that," Noah says. "You'd think I'd have noticed."

"She was pretty gritty when she came in, and the bruising partially obscures it," the nurse says.

"Is it just numbers?"

The nurse pulls the top of the gown down so Noah can see what's there. High on the woman's shoulder, in blue ink, it reads: 2-3-1-9-1-2.

"Do you know what it is?" he asks.

The nurse shrugs. "Nobody seems to have an idea. It's especially odd for a female."

Noah makes a mental note of the numbers then leans in to the patient as he releases her hand. "I'll be back to see you. You take care now."

By the time he gets to the door, Doyle is looking in from the hallway, reminding Noah he still hasn't tended to his original errand.

"Oh," he tells the nurse. "Can you page Dr. Hokeah for me? Mr. Weintraub is determined to leave the hospital, but Doctor hasn't approved it yet."

"I'll take care of it," the nurse says.

By the time he gets back to Silas's room, Cheryl has him sitting on the edge of the bed. Since he's still in his hospital gown, he's not going anywhere for the moment.

"The doc's being paged," Noah announces and then tell them about the woman down the hall. When he gets to the part about the woman's tattoo, Silas perks up.

"What was that?" he asks."

"The Jane Doe we brought in yesterday. She has a tattoo on her shoulder."

Dr. Hokeah walks in, clipboard in hand, shaking his head at Silas like a teacher to a favorite rascal. "You just love making trouble, don't you? Now what's this about getting discharged?"

Silas looks up as though he has forgotten all about that.

"You're not ready to leave yet, Mr. Weintraub. Maybe tomorrow, okay? But while I'm here, I'll do my daily checkup. If you'll lean back in the bed?" Hokeah asks.

Cheryl says, "We'll step out."

"Why don't we run out to the Lawrence cabin while they take care of him?" Noah suggests.

"Yes," Cheryl says. "Silas, we'll drop back by in a little while, okay?"

After they leave, Dr. Hokeah checks his vitals and the cuts Silas suffered during the beating. "This is looking good, sir. I think one more night and you can go home. How does that sound?"

Silas seems preoccupied with something else, however. He suddenly sits up straight in the bed.

"The numbers."

"What's that?" Hokeah says.

"That's me. The numbers, you have to tell them."

CHAPTER THIRTY-SIX

All around Cliff and Katie's cabin, the guttural grind of an industrial-sized backhoe and the continual hum of sump pumps assaults the air.

Cheryl and Noah hear the mechanical cacophony almost a half mile away. "What do you bet Cliff and Katie are in town?" she says over the noise.

Noah nods. "Sure wish I had my ear plugs."

As the red pickup pulls into the driveway, a shadowy figure peeks through the front windows at them.

"That could be Annie Faye," Cheryl says at the top of her voice. As she puts the keys in her side pack, she thinks about the .22 in the glove box. Spur of the moment, she slips it into the pack as well. After all, they are in the country, and heaven knows what kind of critters might get curious.

They give up trying to talk but get out and head to the front door. It's lucky someone has seen them coming, because knocking would be useless.

After a wait, the door opens, revealing Annie Faye Thompson, an ancient, almost blind, woman of color. She stands, squinting at them through thick cataracts and cigarette smoke for a moment, then motions them inside.

She shuts the door behind them and says loudly, "Well,

it's about time. Hell, I was afraid I was gonna be dead before you found me. Come on inside. It's not as bad in the living room."

Cheryl and Noah exchange looks, both surprised to be expected.

"Follow me," Annie Faye says, leading them through expensive southwestern art and leather furniture into the kitchen area. She puts out her cigarette and finds her pack on the counter, lighting another one with shaky hands. This prompts a prolonged coughing fit. After an awkward wait, it subsides.

"You okay?" Cheryl asks.

"Don't you worry about me." She nods at Noah with distaste. "Who's he?"

"My friend, Noah," Cheryl says, still confused. "And I'm . . .."

"I know who you are. But I wasn't expecting him."

"Oh. Well, did Betty call you?"

"Betty? Who's Betty? Miss Katie called me. It don't make no difference. If he's your helper, I can tolerate it. Come with me." She leads them out the back door.

Outside, and this is almost magical to all three of them, the sounds suddenly begin to cut off. First the deafening backhoe, then other engines switch off, one by one. The resulting quiet makes Cheryl's ears ring.

"Whew, thank heavens," she says checking her watch. A little past noon. *Thank the powers that be for lunch breaks.*

Slowly shuffling, Annie Faye shows them out the back French doors. Directly in front of them lies the newly excavated swimming pool, a fancy, curved design. To the left of the designated pool area, a dilapidated tool shed still stands, leaning at a 35-degree angle, an anomaly which must have been part of the original cabin layout.

"Here it is," Annie Faye announces.

"Here's what?" Cheryl asks, completely confused.

"Where the swimming pool will go."

"You think we're here for the swimming pool?" Noah asks.

Annie Faye looks at him like she would some rabid animal and turns instead to Cheryl. "You were supposed to be here two hours ago to bid on the tiles."

"I'm sorry, ma'am," Cheryl says. "You *are* Annie Faye?"

"I reckon I am. Ain't you the tile lady?"

"No, I'm not. My name is Cheryl Jackson, and I came here to see you, Miss Johnson, not to do with the swimming pool. To get some information."

Annie Faye coughs and takes another drag from her cigarette. "You mean I done walked out here for nothing'? I never laid eyes on you. What you want with me?"

"I knew who you were when I was growing up. Everybody knew you worked for the Lawrences. You remember Bud and Ella Mae? My parents?"

"Was you a ball player or something?"

"Yes, ma'am, basketball."

The old woman's body wracks with laughter, which turns into coughing. "Well, why don't you just say so?" She gives Cheryl a close look. "What you want with me?"

"You knew Effie Lawrence, didn't you?"

"Yeah, she's dead, I hear, poor thing. Got killed in a bad way, so I hear."

"So, you knew her?"

"I knowed all of them. Leastways, the ones what come here to the cabin." Annie Faye starts back indoors. "No need to stand out here." They settle around a dining nook table.

"Did you know Ben Lawrence? Her husband?" Cheryl says.

The old woman looks like she just swallowed rancid meat. "That no good tally whacker? What you want to know about him for?"

"I knew Effie real well," Cheryl says. "Loved her, took care of her. But she never talked about him. What was he like?"

"Like any of 'em. I done learned about men, honey, and they barely fit to wipe my shoes on. Effie finally figured out what we all already knowed about husbands. They gonna sweet talk you til you marry 'em. Then they grabs you by the neck and starts yankin' the chain."

A half smile plays around Noah's lips, but he keeps them

zipped. Cheryl presses on. "So, Ben yanked Effie's chain?"

"In the worst way, honey. That poor gal had no idea what she was in for til it was too late. Too sweet to know any better."

"What happened? Did he cheat on her?"

Annie Faye casts a side glance toward Noah. "He's a man, ain't he? If they got two legs and they walkin', they *will* cheat."

"You saw it, then?" Cheryl asks.

"Oh, sure. That snake was up here all the time, some woman or other all over him."

"How soon after they married?"

"Right away, honey." She chuckles grimly. "Ben didn't stand on no ceremony."

"Did you know any of them?" Cheryl asks.

"Too many to keep track of. And that's back when I was just cleaning part time for them. God knows what all else he got up to."

Noah forgets his place. "Besides the women, what did Ben do when he was around?"

Silence. Annie Faye sighs and ignores him, directing her answer to Cheryl. "I was about to decide he might be okay. Then he got to open his mouth."

Cheryl smooths it over. "Sorry, we think maybe Ben buried some money out here. We're trying to run it down."

"Well, except for lovin' it up and party time, only work I ever seen him do was shovelin' around under that old shed."

"Why?" Cheryl asks.

"Said he was makin' himself a wine cellar. Always down there diggin' it bigger."

"Do they still use that old shed now?"

"No, it's a eyesore, Katie says. They're knocking it down to put in the pool. But Benny Boy had big plans. Gonna wire the whole thing up, he says, so's they can read the wine labels. Hauled down enough wiring to light up Main Street." Her laugh is brittle. "Though it was hard to figure how a man what don't drink nothing but vodka needs his self a big wine cellar."

Cheryl shoots a glance toward Noah, who, in his excitement, forgets his place again.

"Any chance we can see it?" he asks.

Annie Faye ignores him but looks at Cheryl. "Do *you* want to see it?"

"Yes, ma'am. That would be nice."

"Well, you seem nice enough. Maybe I can find them stairs again."

CHAPTER THIRTY-SEVEN

Chief Asa Bointy considers Friday morning breakfasts the highlight of his week—meeting up with Gus and Gray Bear, his old army buddies, a trio that could boast of more military awards than their number. Medals of Valor, Purple Hearts and commendations for service above and beyond.

Asa and Gus, his buddy from Indiahoma, both spent time in the infamous Hanoi Hilton. Gray Bear was Special Forces and spent most of his tours behind enemy lines. Everyone still considers him the premier tracker in the area.

Feeling somehow out of rhythm, Asa is grateful for his laid-back companions today. He's been feeling down, too old and fat for the job. Bits of scrambled egg have settled on the front of one of his new uniforms. He thinks about simpler times—police duty at high school sports events, or crowd control for the Natives' many pow wows. Traffic problems, drunk and disorderly all fit in his comfort zone. But murder? With multiple suspects?

He sits smiling at his friends' stories when Joan Cooley, a Medicine Wheel fixture who has worked in the Lawton Library forever, comes up to the table. He sighs, expecting to be peppered with questions about the murder.

"Chief Bointy?" She smooths her skirt and touches the sides of her swept back hair.

The three look up politely. "Morning, Joan, nice to see you." he says.

"I beg your pardon, but do you have a moment?" She licks her lips nervously. "Could we . . .?" She gestures toward her tiny table in the corner, where she's having cinnamon banana pancakes alone.

Bointy sits, tries to get comfortable in the small chair at the table. "Now, you know, Miss Cooley, I can't talk about police business."

She puts her hands up and shakes her head. "No, that's not it. I knew I'd find you here. I came to tell you something."

Asa feels relieved. "Oh, well then, what's on your mind?"

"It was after Miss Jackson was attacked in the library that I got to thinking," she begins. "I was on duty, and, of course, it was just awful."

"She seems to be on the mend," Bointy says, "so we're lucky for that."

"What got me curious later was . . . what had she been looking at on the microfilm? Could it be related? Well, I called Cheryl the next days, and she told me about finding this grainy newspaper mugshot of Goob Edgars just before she was attacked. And I decided to follow through."

Now she has Bointy's full attention. Since Cheryl was attacked in Lawton, not Medicine Wheel, he had left it to their sheriff to handle. Later, when Cheryl and her lawyer had showed up to complain to him, Bointy finally took notice.

Cheryl said the Edgars picture was probably 40 years old

and it was hard to make out distinct features. The Chief could think of nowhere to go with that information, really.

"But it bothered me," Joan goes on. "So, I drive over to the Lawton Police Station—I've got an 'in' there, an old friend who works in records. Of course, they hadn't done anything, but my friend was able to dig up the original mug shot of Goob Edgars from just before he skipped bail."

This stuns Bointy. "My Assistant Chief couldn't find anything going back that far in our jail records." *Wasn't that what Shelby had said?*

Joan goes on. "And he's right there in Lawton's police files, because that's where Goob Edgars was originally arrested, see? All that happened in front of Southwest Memorial, so Lawton P.D. had the original file on him all along."

Bointy cringes at his oversight. Shelby couldn't find the Medicine Wheel records on Goob because they were lost in a basement flood in the 70's. But he didn't know that Edgars was arrested in Lawton. And Bointy didn't either.

"That's great news," Asa stumbles, shaking his head in wonder. "From over forty years ago."

"Isn't it amazing? And I'm thinking, you know what, there's something to this. People don't go around whacking people in the head in the library for nothing."

"Let's hope not," Bointy adds, just for something to say.

"And I know I'm not as good at heritage research as my friend, Bonnie, from Hobart—she just has a gift for that stuff. So, I drive up to Hobart and I tell her, "You're the historian,' I tell her. I can't find anything else about this guy."

"Join the club," Bointy says with an understanding look.

"Bonnie's smart as a whip and can give you the skinny on any Oklahoma outlaw you want. And I show her the mug shot of Edgars . . .."

He leans forward, all ears. He doesn't want to interrupt Jane's flow but wonders briefly if he might be falling in love.

The librarian's face is animated now. "Bonnie's jaw drops. And this is what I came looking for you, to tell you. Bonnie knows him."

Jane Cooley sits back and waits for his response.

One of his feet involuntarily gives a little kick. "Really?"

"Really."

For a librarian, she does love the drama, the Chief thinks. "And . . .?"

"For starters, he died over a year ago in Cache, Oklahoma."

Bointy feels lightheaded. Cache is less than 30 miles away. "Right in our own back yard?"

"That's right. But how would anybody know that? He hadn't used the name Goob Edgars in forty years.

CHAPTER THIRTY-EIGHT

Asa Bointy's mind reels as he sits at his desk listening to Cheryl Jackson's answering machine.

"Hi, you've reached Cheryl's Personal Services. Sorry to miss your call but leave . . .."

"Damn it," Bointy mutters. When she finishes, he says, "Cheryl, it's Chief Bointy. Listen, you need to call me the minute you can. I don't want to scare you, but you could be danger." There's no answer when he calls Noah Frejo, not even an answering machine.

What started out as a pleasant Friday breakfast with the boys has been turned on its head by the information from Joan Cooley. His stomach roils when he thinks of someone closely connected to Goob Edgars in their midst, and for God knows how long.

He can only think of one person who might know who it is. Cracker's store is his next stop. He needs to get Shelby to investigate Goob Edgars, or his pseudo name in Cache, Orville Eskew. He dials the cruiser's mobile phone, but no answer.

The fact that the prospector's nephew had moved to a small town 30 miles away tells Bointy that Goob Edgars never gave up on finding the prospector's coins. But even if he grew a beard and changed his appearance—which he most surely did— it would have been risky to show his face around Medicine

Wheel or the Lawton area. He had to be working with at least one other person.

He knows the librarian and her research buddy are scouring Comanche County records at this very moment, trying to find others who were related or could have known Goob. Without that information, the Chief must consider everyone, either as someone who needs protection, or as the perpetrator.

As he heads out, Bointy double checks his Glock and makes sure he has a backup clip. He had his suspicions before and didn't follow through. This time he plans to be ready for anything.

CHAPTER THIRTY-NINE

Perspiring and straining his doughy body, Cracker is mopping downstairs when he hears the entrance bell ring on the store level. He curses himself for not remembering to lock it. Now he can't just ignore it.

"Be right up," he calls to the level above and hurries cleaning up the area where he kept the woman. Even after wiping it down a second time with soap and bleach, he's still afraid he won't get it all. They have sprays now, he's heard, that show where blood has been, even after it's scrubbed away. He can't miss a single crack.

He hears Bointy's voice from the top of the stairs. "Cracker? You down there?"

"Just a second. On my way," he hollers. There's no choice but to talk to him now, get it over with. But dealing with the Chief won't be hard. If Cracker steers the talk right, he can get Bointy to do most of the talking. After all, Cracker thinks to himself, nobody can massage a conversation better, when he sets his mind to it, than Yours Truly.

He shuffles his sagging girth up the stairs. As he reaches the store level, he is surprised to see the Chief of Police in full uniform and carrying.

"Hi, Asa." He conjures up his happy merchant face. "Sorry, cleaning up after the damn dogs downstairs."

"It's alright," Bointy says with a patient grin. Then his nose crinkles. "Oh yeah, I can smell the bleach."

Cracker spread his arms wide, as if to say, *What're you gonna do?*

"Coffee's not too old. Have a cup?"

Bointy waves his hand. "Don't go to any trouble."

"No trouble, I'm ready for another myself." As he reaches for the pot, his shoulder creaks. "Whew, I'm telling you, this getting old . . . is getting *old*." He chuckles at his own joke and wipes away perspiration with a red work rag. "So, what brings you out on official business today?"

Bointy looks puzzled for a second, then realizes what Cracker is talking about. "Oh, you mean my new uniform?"

"And service weapon, prominently displayed." Cracker's mouth smiles, but not his eyes.

The Chief lightly shrugs that off and sits before beginning. "No, I'm just trying to fill in some gaps here and there. Thinking you might could help."

Cracker pours coffee for both. "Such as?"

The Chief doesn't dance around the point. "Like father, like son, I'm thinking. I'm wondering if you haven't known about this treasure hunt all along."

Cracker studies him, wondering how much he knows and how much he's guessing at. "I just wish my daddy had passed on what he knew before he died."

"I forget just how it was that your dad died. When was that?"

Cracker purses his lips in thought. "He left one morning on one of his digs, hunting some treasure or other, and that was the last me and my mama saw of him. That was '56."

"Who was he working with then?"

"Don't rightly know. You know the old man. Always digging with someone or another."

"I was thinking he was in cahoots with Goob Edgars."

It takes a few moments before Cracker responds. "You talking about the old prospector's nephew now?"

"That's the one," Bointy nods.

"No. No way. Nobody ever heard from Goob again after he . . . didn't he jump bail and disappear?"

"Yeah, but that's not to say he didn't come back around later. Maybe found himself someone here in Medicine Wheel to partner with."

"That might've suited my daddy fine, but if you remember, my mama was as hell bent a Christian as Effie Lawrence herself. No way she would have let my daddy fall in with Goob Edgars."

Bointy tipped his head. "If she knew, maybe. But I've heard that some relatives of Goob's could have been sniffing around."

Cracker is losing his patience. "Where's all this coming

from, Asa?"

"What would you say if I was to tell you that Goob's been living all these years less than thirty miles from here?"

Cracker's eye are unreadable slits. An awkward guffaw rushes out of his mouth.

"Yep," Bointy says. "After he skipped bail, Edgars came back at some point and settled down in Cache, under an assumed name."

"Now you're puttin' me on." Cracker laughs as he casually moves to the cash register across from the coffee area.

"Nope." Bointy cranes his neck around, but he can't follow Cracker's movement without straining his muscles. "Went by the name of Orville Eskew, and nobody the wiser. When he died a year ago, I think his relatives found something in his personal papers to put them on the scent. Or, shoot, maybe they've been his troops on the ground all this time. For years, even. Either way, we're checking right now on who else in his family might be in on it as well."

Cracker tries to hide the panic that flashes in his gut. The Chief is much farther along than Cracker would've guessed.

"I'll be damned," he grunts. "I've spent some time around Cache, and I never heard nothing like that before."

"So," Bointy tells him, "Now I'm just flat out asking. Who have you been working with, Cracker?"

Carefully, Cracker opens a Roitan cigar box he keeps under the register. A syringe inside is filled with etorphine. Originally, Karen had prepared the animal tranquilizer in case

Cracker might need it with the woman.

Bointy continues. "Because I've been thinking about that last time I was by, and you were nervous as hell. The same day they found the Jane Doe on Elk Mountain."

Cracker looks at Chief Bointy's back and gauges the distance between them. Four steps maybe, then jab it in his neck. He will have to restrain him until it takes effect—could take several minutes. Or . . . his eyes wander to the baseball bat he keeps leaning against the counter. *One hit with that, then the injection?*

He's so deep in thought that when Bointy gets up and turns toward him, it stuns Cracker enough that he steps away and tries to hide the syringe behind his back.

"I'm thinking you already know which of Goob's cohorts might be here in town." Bointy's head tilts to try to see what's in Cracker's hand. "What you got there?"

"Nothing."

Bointy had been watching him, though, before Cracker realized it. "Is that a needle, Cracker?"

Cracker considers a lame story about needing it for the dogs, but he knows they're beyond that. He edges his free hand toward the bat.

At the same moment, Bointy, now only a few feet from the counter, slides his hand over his holster and unsnaps the protective strap.

With surprising quickness, Cracker grabs the bat and swings it at Bointy's head before he can draw his Glock.

With a thud, the bat connects with the Chief's neck and shoulder. He stumbles back, drawing his gun. It barely clears his holster.

Bointy fires wild. Cracker grunts and grabs his shoulder in pain. Stunned for a second, he still manages to poke Bointy's stomach with the bat, jabbing him hard enough that the Chief falls backward. He loses his grip on the Glock. It goes sprawling, out of reach, across the wood floor.

Cracker stands over him, wildly swinging the bat. Bointy rocks from side to side to get out of the way. Finally, Cracker raises his arms too high with the bat, leaving his middle open.

Bointy kicks him in the groin, which stops the big man. He groans and stumbles backward.

Given a few seconds to react, Bointy manages to get on his feet and starts to kick and punch Cracker. The pummeling leaves Cracker crouching in a defensive position, trying to protect his shoulder.

Bointy sees the gun. Cracker spots it and moves toward it. Only a few feet from the gun lies the syringe. As Bointy reaches the gun, Cracker grabs the needle and, before the sheriff can fire, Cracker plunges the syringe into the side of his neck. Bointy slumps, unconscious.

Cracker himself loses his adrenalin. His heart is still hammering inside him. It feels like he's having a heart attack. The huge storekeeper collapses on top of Bointy.

Even partly tranquilized, Bointy manages to push Cracker off him. Once free, he crawls on all fours, gets his weapon and stumbles to his feet. On legs of jelly, he starts toward the front door. He clings to the counter, displays—anything that will help keep him on his feet until he can get to the entrance.

Then, only a few yards from the door, Bointy groans and sways.

The last thing he sees before he slides, unconscious, to the floor, is the wooden cigar store Indian, his welcoming hand reaching out, as though trying to help.

CHAPTER FORTY

The abandoned tool shed has a spray-painted red "X" on its side, marked for demolition. When Noah opens the door, dust and cobwebs whoosh up into the air, leaving Annie Faye gasping for breath. It smells of ancient grease and a ton of mouse droppings.

"It's under the floor there somewhere," Annie Fay says. She needs a minute to stop coughing, during which Noah pokes around under a rotting work bench. He discovers a trap door in the floor, obscured under layers of reddish dust.

Noah glances at the old woman, then turns to Cheryl. "You want to ask her if this is the way to the wine cellar?"

"Now you're just bein' a smart ass," Annie Faye snaps. Then she laughs, which sounds like there are pebbles in her throat. "I'm startin' to take a hankerin' to him. Tell him that's the way, alright."

Noah picks up on the game. "Tell her thanks." They all three chuckle, and for the first time, it feels comfortable for him to be here.

Cheryl and Noah clear the wooden bench and grab the trapdoor handle. Dust flies around the little area. Annie Fay backs away so she can catch her breath and continue to smoke.

Noah has to use his pocketknife to cut through a dried seal of mud around the edges. After several yanks, it finally gives. Cool air from below rises into the shed. Sunlight illuminates a steep stair that has rails, although the construction looks shaky to Noah. When he realizes Annie Faye is coming behind him, he turns and speaks to Cheryl, above.

"Handrails are rickety. You might need to give her a hand."

Annie Faye grumbles, "I don't need no help."

Above them, Cheryl raises her hands, as if to say, *I'm not telling her anything.*

"Used to be a light somewhere." The old woman squints down the stairs. "See if there ain't a switch down there."

Feeling around in near darkness, Noah finds it and flips it on. There's a collective gasp when a bare bulb snaps on. Centipedes and spiders scamper from the brightness.

Annie Faye snorts. "Well, shoot fire and save the matches."

The crude light hangs on a single wire and illuminates a natural sandstone area at the bottom of the steps. A few feet in, it turns into a tunnel leading to darkness.

"This is it, Noah," Cheryl says.

All three move cautiously into a naturally formed cave room, where a ratty old sofa and small Formica table form a crude living area. Wooden shelves all around are filled with ancient junk.

"A wine cellar?" Noah snorts. "Yeah. Right." Over the years the room seems to have become a graveyard for tossed items: broken jars and bottles, a rusted bicycle tire, small turned-up motors, paint cans, corroded batteries.

"So, this is what was going on." Annie Faye takes it all in. "Surprised Ben worked this hard."

"Feels like a storm cellar," Cheryl says.

"Smells like cat's ass to me," Annie Faye declares. "I knew it was all hooey."

"Ma'am, why don't you go on up?" Cheryl suggests. "Get out of this stale air."

"I don't need no persuading," Annie Faye says and heads up the stairs. "You let me know when you're through."

Noah notices what looks like an old attic fan. He brushes away dirt and sees **Air Pump** on the front. Close by are sheets of cheap metal, the type used for signage. He discovers three rusty yellow triangles that unfold from the center of a black circle, the standard Civil Defense icon. Underneath, another sign says, **Fallout Shelter.**

Behind him, Cheryl says, "Ben was trying to redo an old Civil Defense shelter?"

"And doing a piss-poor job of it. In the 50's some people sealed off their old storm cellars to use as shelters. But nobody finished this one."

Cheryl goes over to a narrow opening in the wall. She glimpses through it into a cool darkness. The bare bulb by the staircase casts her shadow onto the walls of a tunnel. "Noah. Come see."

"How far does that tunnel go back?" he muses.

"I think somewhere back in there . . . what if that's where Ben hid his treasure?" With a shiver, she unconsciously puts her hand on Noah's arm.

He says, "You could be right."

Noah marvels over a long string of small light bulbs that someone has rigged inside the tunnel. "These are like glorified Christmas lights connected to an extension cord. This had to be Ben's work. It would break every code."

"I'm sure they won't work, not after all this time," Cheryl says.

"The ones by the stairs did," Noah reminds her. The tunnel string hangs precariously on anything available, from natural protrusions in the tunnel wall to rusted nails. "Okay, plug 'em in."

Cheryl does and the string lights up. Some are blinking, some burned out, but they work, and it looks like they light the way back into the tunnel.

"Noah, I've got a good feeling about this."

"Me, too, but let's think this through. I have equipment at home that'll make it safer to check out. Who knows what creatures we might disturb. We'll need a knife and a small gun, at the least. And a rope we can tie off here and take in with us."

"I don't understand."

"If we get lost, we can find our way back out using the rope."

Cheryl doesn't want to admit he's right. "You know, we may never get a chance like this again."

"We can't risk it, Cheryl. You know that."

"I know that, but . . .."

The heavy grind of the backhoe roaring back into action makes them jump. The engineers and workers are back from lunch.

A heavy scraping sound above them, followed by a deep rumble, makes them put their hands over their ears. The ground beneath them starts to shake.

Suddenly, the unthinkable happens. The earthen wall by the stairs cracks and comes toward them, like a road grader pushing dirt on top of them.

The shed above them trembles and shudders and, after a few moments, crashes to the ground. Machinery above them rumbles. It feels like a tank rolling over a cement ceiling.

CHAPTER FORTY-ONE

"Now, Mr. Weintraub, we need to get you back in bed," the nurse tells him.

He's running the halls in his hospital gown, bare rump flapping in the breeze. He has announced to everyone he sees, "I've got to talk to Chief Asa."

"If you go back to your room, I'll find him for you," the nurse promises.

"No, no. I've made a huge mistake." Silas spots Doyle, leaning over the nurse's station, trying to charm some blonde in scrubs. The old man hurries to him. "You'll do."

Silas grabs Doyle's hand as though to push him to the exit. He doesn't even notice Doyle's bandaged nose and bruised black eyes. "Get hold of Chief Bointy. It's a matter of life and death."

"What is?" Doyle asks.

"That woman in the room next to mine. She's, my niece." As his excitement peaks, he can barely breathe.

"Wow. Really?" Doyle seems half curious, half amused.

"Yes, now get cracking."

Assistant Chief Shelby Myers rounds the corner as Silas's volume reaches high decibels. "Silas, what's going on?" He can barely stifle a grin. "You need to get your clothes on first, sir. You're kind of . . . showing yourself there."

Doyle explains. "He says that's his niece in the room next to him."

Shelby gives Silas an indulgent chuckle. "You sure you're not confused from the pain killers? Your niece is in town. I talked to her just before."

Silas pulls him down to his height and speaks in his face. "I don't know who you talked to, but my niece is right next door. You tell Bointy that."

Shelby gives him a patronizing nod. "I'll do that, Silas. I sure will."

"Well, see that you do. And tell Cheryl. Hurry, damn it. Hurry." Silas hurries inside Room 201.

Seeing her barely recognizable face buried in shrouds of white sheets makes him tear up. "I'm sorry, Josey. I didn't know." He turns to Doyle, who follows him into the room. "I never thought to check."

Silas moves to the head of the bed and pulls aside the sheet from her shoulder. There, crudely tattooed are the numbers 2-3-1-9-1-2. She had told him it was in honor of him.

The sight of it overwhelms him. He looks down on his own forearm, at his faded Auschwitz I.D., cruelly stenciled into his skin almost fifty years ago: 2-3-1-9-1-2.

CHAPTER FORTY-TWO

The air is impenetrable. The falling dirt is so thick Cheryl can barely see her hands in front of her. This must be what a mine cave-in feels like, Cheryl thinks.

She feels Noah's hand on her arm, guiding her, both trembling and unable to speak. Miraculously, the tunnel lights are still on. Flickering, but on.

When they get back to the cave room, it's blocked off by boards and collapsed stones. It is also utterly silent.

Above them, the backhoe rips into the soil again, deepening its path. It shifts gears, backs up with a low squeal, dumps its load and charges again.

"Hey! Up there!" Noah yells. "Stop. Stop digging."

"Stop!" Cheryl screams. "There are people down here."

The fallen boards and weight of the soil are too much for them to move out of the way.

****

A mechanical shriek from the backhoe makes Foreman Phil Lawrence and his assistant look up in alarm from their blueprints.

Cursing the buckling motor, the operator jams the machine into a lower gear. The backhoe hits the shed's concrete floor with an ugly, scraping sound. Its hydraulic gears lock in a grinding halt. "What the hell?" the operator yells.

"Turn her off." Phil shakes his head and turns to his assistant. "Why does shit always happen on Friday afternoon?"

"I'll take a look at her." His assistant grabs his tools as the backhoe belches off.

"Hitting cement shouldn't ruin it," the operator tells him, probably with an eye to covering his ass.

"I know." The assistant lets him off the hook. "It's maybe one of those old depression eras well. Thick damn sides, they had."

Foreman Phil watches as the Lawrence's sleek BMW comes toward the cabin. "Great," he mutters, "now I get to wrangle with the she-devil again." Hoping to make it short and to the point, Phil walks toward the car as they pull into the circular driveway.

After hello's he tells them the bad news. "We're probably done for the day if we can't get her fixed."

"Well, damn." Katie makes both the words into two syllables. She stomps inside the house.

"Sorry, Mr. Lawrence, but it could be Monday before we can find a pro to drive out and look at it."

"These things happen," Cliff tells him. "It isn't your fault."

Katie's back at the door, throwing her hands up in annoyance. "Did our colored already leave?"

Phil ignores her slur. "I haven't seen anybody out all day."

"She walked home early, you can bet. Now I'll have to cook, damn it all." Katie stomps back inside.

Cliff shakes his head in exhaustion. "I sure as hell hope she swims in this sonuvabitch if we ever get it done."

CHAPTER FORTY-THREE

Inside Silas's mobile home, the woman who has been calling herself Josey Spangler, throws her things into her single piece of luggage. If Chief Bointy doesn't yet know she's been impersonating the real Josey, that might buy her enough time to get out of Dodge.

iEver since Silas's real niece survived being dumped into the canyon—what a botched murder attempt that was—it has felt like a ticking bomb leading to their discovery. Still, until someone knows for sure their Jane Doe *is* the real Josey Spangler, they've got a chance.

As she has a hundred times before, Karen James pumps herself up. Her bloodline is royal, too, after all. She descended from Frank James's brief dalliance with her great-grandmother, an exotic dancer in Dallas, who adopted the James last name when she found out she was pregnant. Through three generations Karen has been told whose blood was in her veins. If some in the family doubted it, that wasn't her problem. Nobody could keep her from fulfilling her fate.

She feels better after her pep talk to herself, but this is cutting it too close. It's been sort of thrilling to do all this role playing, but now time was closing in on them. He must know that.

The phone rings, causing her to involuntarily jump. After a moment's hesitation, she answers. "Hello?"

"Don't worry, it's me." The sound of his voice is a calming salve. They have that effect on one another, each capable of calming the other when one of them is about to lose it.

"Thank God, baby. I needed to hear from you so bad. What's going on? Are we safe?"

"We're still okay. Stay cool."

"I'm packed. Ready to get out of here."

"Look, I was calling to assure you--we've still got time. I'm taking care of everything. Don't worry."

"Easy for you to say." Karen James hears the annoyance in her tone but doesn't care.

A moment of silence. "I can hear you panicking from here.'

"Because it's done." Off no reply from him, she asks, "Isn't it over?"

"We've got more than one play left. I need you to meet me."

The energy in his voice gives her a leap of faith. "Where?"

CHAPTER FORTY-FOUR

Inside the Lawrence cabin, Katie announces her displeasure with having to cook by loudly slapping the grocery items on the table as she empties the plastic bags. She wants Cliff to join in her denouncement of the "help."

"We have got to get rid of her," Katie says for the umpteenth time. "I'm telling you."

Cliff, already settled into his recliner, would like to ignore her, but knows her mood will just fester if he does. "Aw, Bunny, I . . . you better settle down, or like I've said before, if you can find someone who'll do what she does for what we pay her--"

Katie knows that's true, but still. "She acts like she owns the place." She whisks past him, leaving a trail of musky scent.

He grabs her hand as she goes by him. "Now, you be careful there. Am I going to have to punish you for being a bad bunny?"

That kind of talk always gets her going. She throws a sultry look back over her shoulder. "Oh, no, Daddy." She gives him a mock pout, and her eyes are teasing. "Anything but that, Daddy."

Cliff is relieved, grateful she is so pliable. He pulls her down into his lap and moves his hand between her legs. "Oh, you are so warm there, baby." He knows by now that timing is everything. If he can harness that hot temper and turn her on, the sex that follows still gives him a rush after all their years.

Later, exhausted from the workout, things are good for fifteen minutes. Katie's good moods are often short-lived, however, and as she watches Cliff paddle, barefooted, to the T.V. she scolds him. "Don't leave your socks there on the floor like that. Pick them up."

Cliff shoots her a deadly look. She's about to go too far. Ignoring her command, he says easily, "The Sooners are about on. Are you going to cook those steaks I picked out?"

"Oh, honey, not tonight. I'm exhausted now."

He turns the channel to the football game, where *BOOMER SOONER* blasts from the television. He speaks loudly to her, "Well, what *are* we going to eat then?"

Katie knows when to back off. She rises and, on her way to the kitchen, touches his face and smiles. "Don't worry. I'll figure something out, Daddy."

He moves back to the recliner, puts his socks back on and listens to the pre-game show. He hears Katie holler something from the kitchen.

"What?"

"I said, did you hear that." She comes to the kitchen door.

"Hear what?" he says loudly over the cheering coliseum on the tube.

"Turn the T.V. down," Katie tells him. "I think someone's out there."

He grudgingly lowers the volume, and both stop and listen. Cliff can't hear it. "It's probably just some animal or other rooting around."

She shrugs and moments later appears from the kitchen with two bags of microwaved popcorn.

Stunned that this is all his earlier performance inspired, Cliff sulks. Katie throws him a bone.

"I've got some Turtle Cheesecake ice cream from Braum's."

He likes hearing this, but after a handful of popcorn, he grimaces. "It needs salt."

Suddenly enthralled by the twirlers on T.V., Katie doesn't move. Unbelieving, he gets up and slumps toward the kitchen. As he stands over the kitchen sink, pouring more salt over the popcorn than his doctor allows, Cliff hears something in the backyard.

He shrugs it off. Probably those damn teenagers cruising country roads, blaring those awful rap songs on their boom boxes. No matter how far from town you move, you can't get away from their obscene music. He's always said if he'd had any sense, he would've bought into a hearing aid company. Everybody in the current generation will need one before they are forty.

He moves toward the windows that look over the back yard. The patio lights don't show anything out of the ordinary.

If Cliff had taken a few steps closer to the window, he could have seen Annie Faye, barely conscious, lying on the patio's flag stones. But the game's about to start. It's time to settle back into his recliner.

CHAPTER FORTY-FIVE

Cheryl and Noah look like gray ghosts. The thick dust clings to their skin like sticky hairspray. They wipe their faces with their clothes, but it's impossible to blow out the dirt stuffing up their noses. Coughing makes it worse.

It's hard to tell how far into the tunnel they've come. It seems markedly darker and colder. Spider webs fill entire areas, stretching across the tunnel and up to the ceiling. Noah pulls them out of the way.

Cheryl ducks low to avoid the webs that crisscross the winding tunnel. She loses her balance and trips. She falls hard, landing on her bad knee. Cheryl's leg throbs with pain. But there's nothing else to do but keep going.

Then the tunnel abruptly forks. To the left is pitch dark.

"Maybe a hiding place back in there?" she suggests. Their flashlights show some wall niches, but they're empty.

"If my sense of direction is right, that dark fork cuts back toward the cabin," Noah says. "This right fork heads somewhere beyond the swimming pool."

Cheryl's leg throbs now, she's so tense trying to maneuver on the uneven floor of the tunnel. Noah notices.

"Hey, why don't you rest here, let me check it out. I can move faster alone, anyway," he says.

"No, not on your life."

"Cheryl, you're hurting, I can tell."

"I'll be fine." Off his look, she says, "Don't baby me."

"I wasn't . . . never mind then. Come on."

Twenty feet ahead, they spot the first gold coin.

CHAPTER FORTY-SIX

When Chief Asa Bointy regains consciousness, the first thing he smells is old dog urine which has soaked into the wooden floor. His head feels like he's caught in a bear trap, and the pain around his temples pulsates. The darkness tells him he's been here a while.

Then it hits him, a gestalt that sends him reeling. He's still at Cracker's store. But where's his gun? And Cracker?

The second question is answered when he rolls over on his side. Cracker lies still in a pool of blood, only a couple of feet away. Shaking off his heavy numbness, Bointy tries to crawl his frame toward, hoping he's not dead.

"Hey, hey, hey, take it easy, Chief," someone says and touches his shoulder.

Only then does Bointy realize that other people are also there. The person telling him to take it easy is Dr. Hokeah, who moves to him. "Don't try to get up, Asa."

When his vision clears, Bointy also sees Doyle Lowe just behind the doctor, peering down at him and Cracker on the floor. "Doyle?"

Doyle bends down beside him. His voice sounds like his adenoids are crawling through his throat. "I found you two like this," he says. "What happened?"

"Don't talk yet," Hokeah warns the Chief. "And don't try to get up either."

"Ambulance is on the way," Doyle assures him.

"Why are you here?"

"Oh, Shelby was taking me to jail when he got an emergency call. He let me out and roared out of there with his emergency lights on. I was walking home when I came by here and saw you and Cracker passed out on the floor. I thought you were both dead." Doyle looks upset.

Chief Bointy knows he has things he needs to do but feels too clouded to figure out what comes first. Shelby will have to handle things until he can get his head screwed back on.

The store window suddenly fills with rotating red and blue lights from the ambulance. He hears Dr. Hokeah giving orders to the paramedics. "This one first," he says, and they move to attend to Cracker.

As the doctor talks low to the EMT's, it finally dawns on Bointy that *he* was the one who shot Cracker. Their struggle unfolds in his mind. More flashing lights in the window, a regular Christmas parade, he giggles to himself.

"Is Cracker okay?" Doyle asks as the gurney rolls past him.

"Gunshot wound to the shoulder," Hokeah says.

"And the Chief?"

"He's still out of it, but I can't smell alcohol on him," the doctor says.

"I was drugged." Bointy slurs his answer. He asks the room, "Where was Shelby headed?"

Doyle shrugs. "He just rushed off."

"Help me to the phone," Bointy tells Doyle, who steadies him until they reach the store's phone.

Bointy manages to punch in the Medicine Wheel cruiser's number.

After a few seconds, "Shelby here."

"It's Bointy."

"Where are you? I've been trying to call."

"I'm at Cracker's," Bointy says with a slur. "Come pick me up."

"I'm almost to the Lawrence cabin on an emergency call. They had a cave-in and somebody's trapped." After a beat, Shelby asks, "You there?"

Bointy isn't sure what to do next. "Do they know who it is?"

"They think it's their hired help. That old lady."

"Okay, on my way." He hangs up and tells Doyle. "My cruiser's parked by the door. I need you to drive me somewhere.

"Sure." Doyle nods vigorously, perked up about getting behind the wheel of a police cruiser.

A couple of minutes later, Doyle helps Bointy inside the cruiser, waving at the doctor and medics like he's supposed to be doing this. Once inside, Bointy smells a whiff of alcohol. "Doyle? Are you drunk?"

"Just a little. I've driven worse off, though." Doyle starts the car before Bointy can say anything else.

Even through his grogginess, the Chief already wonders how many ways he's going to regret this. "Well, at least it's dark."

"Where to?" Doyle asks, like a chipper taxi driver.

CHAPTER FORTY-SEVEN

Dirty and partially obscured by the dusty tunnel floor, the ancient gold coin still radiates dignity. Ornately carved, an unknown god's visage engraved in the center, the coin feels heavy in Cheryl's hand. She rubs her fingers over the surface, clearing the surface of dust and mud. Its shine reflects off the tunnel lights.

"This looks exactly like the one Ben Lawrence gave Patty Boney."

Noah squeezes her arm and supports her as they move ahead.

"Look, up here, there's more," he says. Coins dot the tunnel's path, as though someone in a rush had spilled them out of a basket. They move ahead without speaking, excitement overcoming them, picking them up as they go.

Noah examines another coin, then says, "Wait, this isn't . . .."

"What?" Cheryl studies it. "No, that looks like a gold button."

"From a uniform?" Noah looks to see if she's thinking the same thing.

She nods. "Military."

"Yep." Even more cautiously, they start down the path again. Around the next curve they glimpse a military dress shoe.

A skeletal foot still rests inside it. The full view takes their breath away.

A shrunken, mummified body, lying on its side, wears the moth-eaten remnants of an Army uniform, circa 1950. A .45 automatic is by his side. More gold Mexican coins sprinkle the area around him.

"That's Effie's husband. Must be," Cheryl says after a moment.

Noah kneels beside the body and examines the coat. "How did you die, Ben?" Then he finds two holes with burned edges. "Look."

"Who did that to him?" Cheryl looks farther into the tunnel. "Look, more coins up ahead." Her aching leg is forgotten.

"That also means there's another way out of here, up ahead somewhere."

Their exhaustion and dry throats, the dirt that covers their bodies, all fade now as a new surge of adrenalin hits them both. Cheryl stares down at Ben's mummified frame.

"Think he was headed out to pick up Patty Boney?"

"Yeah. And picking up his hidden treasure on the way." Noah looks at the scattered coins in front of them. "But if Ben was shot here, who dropped the ones up ahead?"

They set out cautiously, following the coins like breadcrumbs leading the way. The trail becomes thicker, as though the weight of carrying the heavy coins had proved too much for someone.

They are literally walking over a carpet of coins when they come upon the second skeleton.

CHAPTER FORTY-EIGHT

When Shelby arrives in the cruiser, an ambulance is running, lights blazing in the Lawrence's driveway. Its rotating lights flash red and blue on the house's front window. He knows it's gutsy cutting things this close, but thinks he can pull it off.

Behind the house, two paramedics administer to Annie Faye, who was unconscious on the patio flagstones when Cliff and Katie finally found her. Under the eaves, Katie watches and wrings her hand.

She spots Shelby Myers coming toward the commotion. "Oh, thank god you're here, finally."

"Who's hurt?" Shelby asks.

Katie gives him a quick rundown of her seeing the old woman outside and calling the ambulance. "We couldn't get hold of Chief Bointy." In a lower, concerned voice, she asks him, "Can Annie Faye sue us, Shelby? I don't think we have Worker's Comp."

"I got no idea, Katie." Shelby looks around for Karen.

Cliff spots them and hurries that way. "What a damn disaster. I left a message with my contractor, but he hasn't gotten back to me. I will sue his ass from here to--"

Shelby interrupts. "Was the old lady the only one down there?"

Cliff and Katie look at each other. This hasn't occurred to them.

"She was the only one here," Cliff manages to say.

"No," Shelby corrects him. "The hospital said Noah and Cheryl were out here, too." He moves quickly toward Annie Faye's gurney and speaks around the medics who are tending to her.

"Who else was down there with you?"

Annie Faye struggles through the fog of her injuries to remember. "That Indian . . . he's down there. And his girlfriend."

"Noah? Cheryl Jackson?" Shelby asks.

"They were looking around for somebody . . . ."

The medic cuts her off. "Here we go, ma'am. You're going to feel real relaxed in about a minute." They wheel off the gurney toward the ambulance.

A new pair of headlights flashes across their faces as Karen/Josey's Camry pulls up to the side of the house. She jumps out and heads toward the Lawrences.

"Josie," Katie says when she sees her. "What are you doing here?"

"Cheryl, my client, is out here somewhere. I heard there was a cave-in."

"How did you know about that?" Cliff asks.

"Are you kidding?" Karen/Josie says, trying to improvise something that doesn't blow her cover. "The whole town knows by now." Karen looks toward the cave-in. "How do I get down there?"

Cliff points to the original entry under the shed. "I think they've almost opened it up over there—where the shed was."

Karen hurries in that direction and sees the newly dug hole, freeing the blockage caused by the backhoe. Light flickers from underneath, as if seen through a carved pumpkin.

A moment later Shelby sees her and moves to her side. She asks in a low voice, "Where does that go?"

"Not really sure," he answers, trying to look businesslike. "They think it's stairs down to some old cellar entrance. I need to check it out."

"That's my client down there," Josey insists for anyone hearing them. "I'm going with you."

He glances at her, a smile playing around his lips. "Good idea."

CHAPTER FORTY-NINE

By the time Doyle wheels the cruiser down the cabin's long driveway, Bointy's drug-addled head feels a little clearer. Leaning out the passenger window and letting the cold night air blast him in the face has also helped.

Red and blue emergency lights slice through the dark sky. It's an ambulance, he realizes, lit up and speeding straight toward them on the narrow asphalt drive.

Doyle's eyes widen. "That ambulance just pulled out from the cabin." He glances at Bointy. "Should we turn around and follow them?"

"No, got to see what's happening at the cabin first." The cruiser phone rings, and Bointy grabs it. "Bointy here."

Silas's voice booms with static through the speaker. "Chief. Finally. Why didn't you call me?"

"Call you?" Bointy has no idea what he's talking about. "Was I supposed to?"

"Haven't you talked to Shelby?"

"Yeah. A while ago."

"Damn it." Silas sounds furious. "He was supposed to tell you."

The flashing ambulance blurs past them. Then, only the

cruiser's bouncing headlights illuminate the road ahead, to the Lawrence cabin.

Thinking that he can't get into a long Silas rant right now, Bointy asks, "Tell me what, Silas?" They approach the circular drive of the cabin, and the conversation only confuses him.

"I found her in the hospital," Silas shouts into the phone. "I told Shelby to tell you. It's not the same one."

Bointy, now completely lost, shouts back, "What? I can't understand you, Silas."

"I said, Cheryl's lawyer is not the one."

Finally, Bointy gets it. The poor man is having a morphine episode, seeing conspiracies everywhere. "Okay, Silas, I'll take care of it," he lies. "Don't worry about a thing."

"I'm telling you; I saw the numbers on my niece's shoulder." Silas sounds desperate now.

Doyle whips the cruiser into the circular drive. Bointy speaks loudly into the phone. "Got to go. It's an emergency, Silas. Have to call you back." He hangs up.

Doyle looks over at him.

Bointy explains, "Silas is seeing things."

They get out and hurry to the back yard, with Doyle helping the chief to stay balanced. "Cliff! What's going on?" Bointy asks.

Cliff pulls them to the cave-in spot and tells them about Annie Faye's rescue. "And just now, Shelby and Cheryl's lawyer went down there to find Noah and Cheryl."

Doyle looks stunned. "Cheryl's under all that?"

"What in hell were they doing down there?" Bointy demands.

"You got me," Katie announces sullenly. She hurries toward the house. "Everybody around here has gone flat out nuts."

Bointy's head is feeling clearer now. "Wait, you say Shelby took Josey down there?" He thinks of Silas's cryptic phone call, and suddenly is not so sure of himself. But before he can think it through, Doyle interrupts his thoughts by rushing toward the gaping dirt hole.

"I've got to get down there."

Bointy's voice stops him. "Hold your horses. I need you up here. Nobody's heading down there halfcocked." Bointy turns to Cliff. "Call the Fire Department. We need them and tell them to bring Al and Joe Bob. And to put out an alert for volunteer rescue workers."

Cliff nods and heads to the house.

Bointy calls after him. "Tell them to bring shovels."

CHAPTER FIFTY

Cheryl's bad leg has turned into a painful throb. Yet it feels numb, so she keeps stumbling as they try to move on. Noah insists she sit, and he tries to massage it.

"I'll just rest it a minute. It'll be okay," Cheryl is frightened, but the feeling will come back, she tells herself. She doesn't want to scare him.

It doesn't look like he believes her, but he says, "I'll just take a quick look ahead. You keep massaging that knee."

Cheryl gets into her side pack and finds her pain pills. She bites on her tongue to try to rouse some saliva, but in the end, she's forced to chew them. She's relieved to notice the little .22 inside the pack.

It's less than a minute before she hears him say, "Oh my god."

"What?" She pulls herself up and goes that way.

Around the next turn, she finds him kneeling over the second mummified skeleton. What's left of a plaid flannel shirt and overalls cling to the remains of a large body. Work-worn, steel-toed boots cover the feet. A big boney hand still holds a .45.

Noah voices a quiet grunt, then looks up at her. "Cheryl, this was a gunfight to the death down here."

"Old man Cracker?" She sits and checks Cracker's pockets. "Here we go," she says, lifting out a wallet. She pulls out a dusty, ancient Oklahoma Driver's License, issued to Jacob Box, Sr. of Medicine Wheel. She hands it to Noah. "Sure enough. This is Cracker's dad."

Noah shows her two shell casings in his hand. "These were in his side pocket. He probably picked them up after he shot Ben."

"From his own .45?"

"He must have found out Ben was taking off with the money. And came after him." Noah puts his arm around Cheryl's waist and helps her to her feet.

"We need to get you out of here," he tells her. "Can you feel your leg?"

She sidesteps his question. "It's okay. I can do it."

"Hang on to me, I'll support this side." He pulls her up and helps her walk.

A faint call from behind them echoes through the walls. "Cheryl? Noah?"

"Is that Shelby?" Cheryl asks.

"Are you two down here?" Shelby calls out again.

"We're back here," Noah calls out, then tells Cheryl, "They must have cleared that opening where we first came in."

"We're heading toward you," Noah shouts.

When Noah and Cheryl come back by Ben's body,

Shelby already stands there, his weapon drawn. Behind him, Josey/Karen points a snub-nosed revolver at them. At the sight of Ben's skeleton, she slips it into the back of her jeans, then moves to the body, hand to her lips in shock.

"Is that . . .?" she asks. "Who is that?"

"Ben Lawrence, Effie's first husband," Cheryl says.

Karen picks up some of the ancient coins and grabs Shelby's arm. "This is it. We found it." She gives him a quick hug, then starts to pick up loose coins and jam them into a leather bag.

There's a different energy between her and Shelby that Noah and Cheryl haven't seen before. Now it seems obvious. It's intimate, knowing, *attached.*

"Hurry," Shelby says, picking up gold coins as well. "We've got to keep moving."

"There's another body just ahead," Noah says, stalling.

Shelby asks, "Who?"

"His wallet says it's Cracker's dad."

"Show me." Shelby motions with his gun for Noah to lead the way. As they go, he turns back to Karen. "Keep an eye on her."

"Hurry," Karen says. "We're running out of time."

The men disappear.

"What are you two talking about?" Cheryl asks her.

"You just shut up," Karen tells her and keeps raking up the coins. "I've had a gutful of putting up with you." Her face takes on a cold harshness.

Loud, angry words between the men carry to back to the women. "What the hell?" Karen mumbles.

Shelby sounds loud and pissed off. "Keep moving, damn it."

"No, not unless you let Cheryl go."

"I'll shoot you right here. How would that be?" His voice is ugly.

Noah's bluff is just as cold. "Do that, you'll never get out of here."

The women listen as the argument turns into the slams and blows of a full-on fight, which echoes down the tunnel to them.

Cheryl grips her shoulder strap and maneuvers her hand to inside her pack.

A gunshot booms down the tunnel. Her heart freezes. Noah cries out in pain, then yells. "Get out, Cheryl. Run. Run."

Instead, she pulls the .22 from her pack.

By the time Karen stands up and reaches for her weapon, Cheryl has the .22 aimed at her.

"Stop right there." Cheryl warns her.

Karen freezes and slowly puts her hands out so Cheryl can see them.

A falling rock causes Cheryl to glance away.

In the same instant, Karen rushes Cheryl and kicks her in the face. The gun flies. Then Karen pummels every place her foot can reach—Cheryl's stomach, legs, head.

Cheryl fends off the attack with her hands, but she can't slow the assault. Karen is too quick and agile on her feet.

After the first rush of kicks, however, Karen aims too high and loses her balance for a second. Seeing her chance, Cheryl locks onto Karen's foot and pushes it back toward her. With a grunt, Karen goes down, the air knocked out of her. Cheryl spots her .22 and grabs it.

She almost has it firmly in hand, when she hears a loud crack and feels the whack of something hitting her head. She can feel blood flowing into her hair. She has a hazy glimpse of Noah pulling himself toward her. Then, in an instant, everything goes black.

CHAPTER FIFTY-ONE

Doyle has moved down inside the cavern, past the Civil Defense Shelter and has started down the lighted tunnel.

"Cheryl! Noah! You guys down here?"

He sees a flashlight coming his way. "Hello? Cheryl? Is that you?"

Shelby and Karen are near the exit that's now shored up by the rescuers. They hear Doyle Lowe's calls. He stops and whispers to Karen. "Follow my lead." She nods.

A few steps farther, they run into Doyle. "You guys okay?" he asks.

"We're good," Shelby assures him.

"Are Cheryl and Noah back in there?"

Karen says, "They're back there a bit. We're going for help."

"Yeah, we all were hurt from the earlier cave-in," Shelby says.

Doyle says, "Okay, I'll head that way. Send a medic and a couple of guys from the Rescue Team."

When Shelby and Karen make it to the original space under the shed, Chief Bointy is there directing traffic and trying to get everyone to move back.

"We don't know what this thing's going to do next. They've got it temporarily braced for now, but we need everybody to stay clear of this area."

Shelby is stunned to see his boss. He wonders how he can be on his feet after that horse tranquilizer Cracker gave him. But he manages to look upbeat.

"Chief, you okay? I thought you'd be in the hospital."

Bointy says, "I'll get around to it. What's going on down there?"

"Noah's hurt, can't hardly walk. Cheryl fell . . . we were just coming back to get help for them." Shelby indicates Karen. "Josey's a little shook up," he explains as he pushes past the chief.

"I'm having trouble breathing," Karen says and begins to cough.

"We were going to run her back to town to get an inhaler she uses."

Bointy says, "No, Shelby, I need you here." He motions to a medic with the ambulance. "Go see him. He'll have what you need."

Karen stalls, glancing at Shelby, who is weighing the situation. Bointy eyes them carefully.

Shelby touches Karen's arm and whispers, "Don't blow it now." Then he looks toward the medic. "Go on. What can it hurt?"

"I'll be right back," he assures Bointy.

He takes Josey's arm, and they walk toward the ambulance, but Bointy is soon distracted by people needing instructions.

Josey tells Shelby, "Okay, he's not looking now. The Camry's right over there. See? Let's just head that way."

"If Bointy sees us, we'll make a run for it to the car." They move from a normal walk to faster and faster, all the while trying to look normal and going about their business.

But nobody realizes what's going on. People are too busy, doing what they've been asked to do.

They throw the bags of coins into the car, quickly climb into the Camry, and in a flurry of activity back out onto the road. Shelby speeds away, with Karen leaning over the back seat to see if they have company.

Karen screams at the top of her lungs. "We're clear. No one even noticed us." Then they both are hollering. She hugs him so tight he can barely steer.

"Home free!" Shelby bellows.

CHAPTER FIFTY-TWO

When Asa Bointy gets off the phone with Jane Cooley, he stands and looks around the activity at Cliff and Katie's place with a disjointed sense of reality. Rescuers are digging and putting wood supports around the entrances they're clearing. Locals hustle from one group to the other, offering help, shovels, bottled water and flashlights.

But Shelby and Josey/Karen are gone, slipped away in her Camry, right under his nose. The chief fights tears and has to cough and clear his throat so no one will notice.

When a 70's pickup pulls up to the cabin, Gus and Gray Bear get out, looking for their breakfast buddy. They spot him sitting on a box by the original cave-in. The Chief has to swipe his cheeks as they hurry over to him. They don't have to say much. They've been tuned in to one another for decades.

"What can we do?" Gray Bear asks.

Gus puts his arm on Asa's shoulder. "Figured you could use some help."

"They have everything in hand now," Bointy says, "But I just got some news. Let's find somewhere private." They find three folding chairs in the garage and make a small circle.

"First off," Asa says, "We've been conned. The whole town has been conned. You know Jane Cooley, the librarian, don't you?" They nod. "A friend of hers has been digging around about the Frank James treasure for years."

Gray Bear nods, familiar with it through his grandfather.

"So, Jane called me just now to bring me up to date. They tracked down some of the old prospector's descendants. Jane's friend had an 'in' with someone who could look at Lawton's police files."

Gus and Gray Bear lean forward in anticipation.

"Goob Edgars—he was Charlie's young, hotheaded nephew—beat up the doctor who treated old Charlie. They caught and convicted him, but Goob jumped bail and disappeared."

"He went after everybody who had treated the old prospector, didn't he?" Gus asks.

"Yep." Asa checks his notes. "This is the new stuff they found out. Eventually, Goob located everyone on the hospital staff who was around that night and beat them up or worse. Except he could never chase down Effie Lawrence because she wasn't there to find.

"Effie had left her hospital job to join the military as a nurse. And she had a different last name because she had just married Ben Lawrence. They both served the next two years abroad during the war."

Gray Bear shakes his head at the absurdity of it. "Goob threatened all the medical staff that worked the night the prospector died, but he missed the one person who had personally tended to him?"

Asa says, "Here's the shocker. Goob skipped bail—we all

knew that—but after that he himself dropped out of sight and bided his time."

Gus nods. "People made bets on where he'd gone, my father says."

"And now, finally, we know. Sometime after he got away from the law, Goob changed his name and hid in plain sight."

"Around here, you mean?" Gus asks.

"According to Jane and her friend, he took the name 'Orville Eskew' and settled down in Cache. Lived there over 30 years." Gray Bear and Gus are stunned.

"Less than thirty miles away?" Gray Bear repeats it in disbelief.

"His family of nieces and nephews hung around there for years, waiting for him to share what all he knew about the treasure. But the old man apparently decided they couldn't be trusted. Goob turned into a stubborn, miserable coot over the years. He became senile before he could tell anybody what he knew. By the end, he was deluded *and* paranoid. He accused them of planning to kill him."

"Never showed them his journals and notes?" Gus has no words for this. "Not even to blood relations?"

"The librarian found that the cause of death was dementia," Asa said. "He died last year."

Gray Bear clucks his teeth. "The family didn't get a look at Goob's papers and journals until after he died."

"That's not clear. Jane and her friend think the Edgars—

or the 'Eskews'--couldn't wait. They put one of Goob's ambitious nephews to work *before* he died."

"Who?" Gus asks.

"Shelby Myers. That's what Jane was calling to tell me. Not only was Shelby Goob's great-great nephew, or something like that, but his wife, Karen, claims to be an illegitimate daughter of Frank James. She's slick as snot herself and played like she was Josey Spangler. That solved the problem of Silas's niece coming to town."

Nobody says anything for a few moments as they try to process all the pieces.

"Where's this Karen been?" Gray Bear asks.

"Living in Lawton." Bointy rubs his face with his hands. "This is a damn nightmare."

CHAPTER FIFTY-THREE

When Doyle helps Noah and Cheryl climb out of the original shed entrance, people clap and yell for all three of them. A generator spotlight splashes the scene in bright white. Two medics with a stretcher secure Noah and take him to a waiting ambulance.

Cheryl can walk, technically, but her head wound is concerning. Gus and Gray Bear half-support, half-carry her to the same ambulance. Doyle follows along carrying their packs and jackets.

Cheryl and Noah are checked out using the onboard medical equipment. Al, one of the rescuers, talks with the medics and warns Cheryl to stay awake, in case she has a concussion. As for Noah, he'll need surgery on his gunshot, but it passed through his thigh without hitting any blood vessels.

By the time they are set up inside the ambulance, the I.V. painkillers are taking effect.

Chief Bointy comes to the back of the ambulance. "They'll be waiting for you at the hospital." He is putting on a brave face, but he looks beaten to Cheryl. Maybe it's been too many blows in one night.

"What are the chances they're still in the area?" Noah asks.

Bointy shakes his head. "We put out APBs on Karen's

silver Camry, but it's almost dark."

"We'll get them, Chief." Cheryl hears how hollow it sounds.

Gus and Gray Bear join Bointy and comfort him in low voices. Bointy finally looks at Cheryl and Noah. His tired eyes want to promise something. "This isn't over." He looks down the dark night road. "Today, him. Tomorrow, me."

They take off toward Southwest Memorial. Silas will be there, Cheryl realizes, and she can finally meet his real niece. And maybe she'll be lucky enough to see Cracker handcuffed to his hospital bed . . . without a cigarette.

Yet as grateful as Cheryl feels to be alive, to have Noah safe, she feels cheated, beaten, as disillusioned as a wind torn flag. It eats at her gut, the thought that down some dark highway, Shelby and Karen are laughing at them, getting away. They murdered her sweet Effie, and nobody can get at them now.

If there is any justice . . . she thinks. But if there is anything she knows in this imperfect world, it's that often there is *not* justice. Only angry despair. And right now, Cheryl isn't sure how anybody lives with that.

CHAPTER FIFTY-FOUR

Six months later

The locals don't talk about it much, but most were disappointed in Asa Bointy's last two months as Police Chief. A lot of people think he just lost heart, that he never recovered after the most notorious outlaws of his career disappeared down a dark road last fall.

Shelby Myers and Karen James had driven away from the Lawrence cabin the night of the cave-in and, other than a couple of possible sightings in southern Texas, had simply vanished.

One of Bointy's last duties was to oversee Cracker Box Jr.'s plea deal with the state. According to the scuttlebutt, Cracker gave them everything he knew, but it still wasn't enough to find the guilty couple, or the money.

Soon after, the Chief handed over the legal reins to up-and-comer "Heck" Hardin, a good kid from Lawton. People seem to like him, even though he doesn't take as much time to visit during his usual rounds, the way Asa always did. The new Police Chief has taken some of Bointy's cues, though.

Just showing up at the Big Chief Diner for breakfast every morning has earned him fifty percent approval ratings. In fact, this Friday morning "Heck" sits with Bointy and the Breakfast Club, back in their usual spot after an extended fishing trip.

Asa, Gus, and Gray Bear are sitting particularly tall this morning, visiting with locals they haven't seen in their several weeks' absence. One has to look past the sweatshirts and jeans to imagine their ancestral warriors, but there is something special in their demeanor this morning.

Cheryl and Noah enjoy a hot skillet breakfast, a celebration of her six-month sobriety chip. She is in the process of moving out to Cliff and Katie's cabin, which officially became hers a month ago.

One nice thing about small towns is that estates can be settled more quickly, and Judge Chibitty closed out Effie's legal entanglements in record time. Cheryl came out with enough money to really set herself up, while Cliff managed to avoid fraud but now spends his days working regularly at the John Deere store, much to Astrid's dismay. And Katie's as well, who had to cut back on her cherished Botox treatments.

Lots of people have been waiting for Cheryl and Noah to either tie the knot or move in together. Both like having their own places too much. Not that they don't spend most nights together wherever is most convenient.

As they finish their plates and start on one last cup of coffee, Silas struts in with an armful of newspapers and a huge grin on his face. They wave him over. He distributes the papers to all the tables as he heads toward their booth.

"Have you heard?" Silas asks them as he slides into their booth.

"Something on the Native Center?" Noah asks. He has recently been recruited to help plan and build a new Plains Indian Tribes Museum.

"Yeah, did they find who was the big mystery donor?" Cheryl asks.

"No, that's old news. You've got to keep up," Silas chides her.

"What then?" Noah asks.

Silas pushes The Lawton Chronicle over to them as he sits down. "Front page. Look."

Cheryl and Noah's eyes pop. A picture of Shelby Myers in uniform, beside an early mug shot of Karen James are huge on the page. Her heart pounds at the headline: **Escaped Former Lawman and Wife Found Dead.**

"Read it, Cheryl," Silas insists.

She begins. *"Former Medicine Wheel Assistant Chief of Police, Shelby Myers, and his wife, Karen James, who have been missing since their involvement in the brutal death of Effie Lawrence six months ago, were found murdered in a beach house on the Mexican coast two days ago."*

Cheryl looks up at Noah, who is as stunned as she is. People push her to keep reading. *"The Coroner in Mazatlán has not revealed the manner of death but said both had been dead for several days before being discovered by a guide who had been booked to take them on a deep-sea fishing trip."*

"Talk about karma," Noah says in a low voice.

"Yep," Silas says. "Fate. Pure and simple. It caught up with them."

"What about the money?" Cheryl asks as she goes back

to the story. *"No suspects have been arrested. The Mazatlán Police state that they are still interviewing people in the area. The couple had recently moved into the remote beach area, but few of their neighbors knew them."*

"Get to the part about the money," Silas insists.

She skims down the article a few inches. "Oh, here. *There was no evidence of the rare Mexican coins that the couple was accused of stealing, and no accounts or deposit boxes belonging to the couple have been recovered.*

Everyone soaks it in for a moment. Then Noah gives a low chuckle. "I guess sometimes life balances the books for us."

Quickly, the diner is buzzing with the news. It's difficult to hear over the din. Cheryl looks pointedly over at the Breakfast Club. Gus and Grey Bear are looking over the story, but Asa Bointy is staring right back at her, the hint of a smile on his lips.

Her heart starts to pound as she understands. Then he deliberately hoods his eyes and slowly opens them again. It is so slight anyone could have missed it. But Cheryl knows what it means. They will never speak directly of it, nor of all the anonymous, enormous donations that have started pouring in for Native causes and new schools.

Then Cheryl and Chief Bointy smile warmly at one another, and she finally understands his cryptic message of six months ago: *"Today him, tomorrow me."*

THE END

Reader Reviews for Linda McDonald-s Books

COLD

"Shirley Loomis Bass is a most unlikely heroine in this beautifully told tale of suspense and intrigue. She's middle aged and overweight, with no confidence in her physical capacity. But she finds reserves of strength and will not only to survive against all odds, but to save another person and to find love in their shared experience. Linda McDonald has written another book full of fascinating characters and an intriguing plot that makes the reader reluctant to take even a short break from the story. Her attention to detail is perfectly balanced between too much and too little. Her descriptions of characters and environment capture the imagination and make the reader feel involved in their adventure. I can hardly wait for her next book!"

"This was interesting from page one through to the end. The story keeps on track without digressing into complicated psychological profiles or detailed history lessons about the Alaskan wilderness. There was plenty of character development, color, action, plot and "ambiance" all intelligently expressed as the story unfolded. An excellent read. Pure, moving and to the point. I'm looking forward to reading more of Linda McDonald."

Anticipation Plus! Wow.

I love a fun read and Linda McDonald fills the bill. Her experience as a dramatist and actor gives the characters wonderful motivation, and her ability with descriptive language allows the reader to not only see and hear what is going on, but to smell and feel it as well. This book has been on my Kindle for several months and I've put off starting it, because I knew once I started, I would not be able to get anything else done until I was finished. Thank you, Linda, for your hard work and genius. Your books thrill and delight.

IN A WORLD OF HURT

Great Book from Beginning to End! Great character development and mystery construction. The story encompasses a murder mystery, legal thriller and romance. I enjoyed every page.

Great Mystery! Twists and Turns that keep you reading. This is one of those mysteries that makes you care about the strong lead character, Ellababe, and keeps you wondering how it will all work out for her til the very end. There's an interesting cast of characters around her, including her dog, Jake, as she deals with starting her life over after a tough divorce, then dealing with the fallout of her ex-husband's mysterious disappearance. Detective Ortiz adds some scary experiences as he explores what happened. Really enjoyed this story! You won't want to put it down once you get started!

CAUTION! - Don't start reading this book if you are short of time because you won't want to put it down!!!! Well written, timely and suspense filled with complex but relatable characters. Seriously, it's a great mystery.

Couldn't put it Down! Excellent Read! Linda McDonald never disappoints!! Heck of a story with relatable and well-defined characters. Another thought provoking, nail-biting whodunit that kept me up too late reading a few nights!! Loved it!!

IN THE LION'S MOUTH

Texas, Sun, Sand and Surf—What could go Wrong? Carrie Jo Murray is not your average 20-something and Linda McDonald is not your average author spitting out whodunits or suspense novels with the usual list of good and bad characters. There is nothing average in her books. This novel also involves a Winnebago, also not your average get-away vehicle. I love the character Leo Marvins (nice play on a very well-known action hero there) as well as his Viet Nam cronies and Leo proves to be more than a good guy; a great guy with a lot of post-Marine survival smarts, something her boyfriend, Jason, definitely is not. But Leo is complicated, many faceted and more than your average beach-bum from Boca Chica in Texas. More scenes heat up than the Texas temperatures. Don't take anyone at face value. No one and nothing is as it seems...lots of interesting characters, plot twists--I didn't trust any of them. I don't think I was supposed to! This is the second McDonald book I've had the opportunity to download. I also read "Here Comes the Night" (excellent--and the reason I jumped on this one). The two can't really be compared. What stays consistent is the quality of her writing, the depth of the story, and the insight into the characters. You don't see most of these plot twists coming--and if you can't predict the storyline--you gotta stay tuned to find out what really happens. I recommend you do!

Absolutely Loved This! I don't give many five-star ratings, but this had me anxiously reading way into the nights to see how it all came out. Two different scenarios, weapons dealers and drug runners tie together so nicely in the end. You don't know who is with whom while you're reading through the twists and turns. You will come to love the two main characters, who have been thrown together accidentally to cooperate in trying to solve the mystery of the situation they find themselves in. They are always in a fix of one kind or another, as the story fascinatingly unfolds. Many other colorful characters come to light to round it all out perfectly. The cartel is a tough bunch to deal with, having no mercy for anyone. Great story; talented author. Get this book and enjoy a couple of relaxing days, being thankful you're not in the characters' shoes yourselves for real!

Made in the USA
Monee, IL
10 September 2023

42476345R00154